SPACE ROGUES

THE EPIC ADVENTURES OF WIL CALDER, SPACE SMUGGLER

JOHN WILKER

Cover art by Anthony Tanaka

ISBN: 978-1-7326287-1-7

V. 8.1

❀ Created with Vellum

Mega thanks to the following people:
Nicole Wilker — My loving wife who tolerates my weirdness
Tom Ortega — Who helps keep me focused on the target
Jeffry Houser — Who is awesome at poking holes in my ideas for the
better

... And, of course, my folks!

You're about to embark on a fun adventure!

When you're done reading, I hope you'll take a minute to leave a review!

PART ONE

CHAPTER 1

JAILBREAK

The two prisoners, surrounded by almost a dozen Partherians, walk down the corridor of the battleship. There's no mistaking its design as Partherian: octagonal halls with harsh white lighting and bare metal grates for the floor, a faint odor of moss. The entire entourage is making their way towards the small prisoner's galley for the prisoners' afternoon meal.

"Excuse me," a voice from behind the group.

As the group turns, prisoners and jailers alike, they come face-to-face with a single biped standing in the corridor. The stranger is wearing a long brown coat over some type of spacesuit with integrated body armor. Their head is completely covered by a form-fitting helmet and face-mask. The entire faceplate is mirrored and outlined in a blue glow.

The intruder raises two pulse pistols into the air—blasts ring out, dropping six of the Partherian guards. As the rest scatter, the two prisoners fall to the floor, the metal grating pressing against them. The stranger is still standing in the center of the corridor, the faint sparkle of a personal energy shield visible. Blaster bolts are striking the shield, causing it to ripple and flicker. The personal shield is absorbing more hits than most off-the-shelf models are capable of—it's clearly a modified version meant to handle serious abuse.

The mystery figure leaps from one side of the corridor to the other, then runs straight at the remaining guards, leaping up and over them, firing with every step, guards dropping left and right. Within ten seconds, the remaining Partherians are unconscious.

"You know, you could have helped," the stranger says, moving to stand over the two prisoners, who are still lying prone and partially hidden by an unconscious Partherian.

The prisoners crawl out from under their previously conscious captor. "With what—our shackled hands? A harsh rebuke maybe?" the female prisoner asks, frowning as she helps her companion up. "Who are you? What are you? What do you want?"

Both prisoners are wearing standard Partherian prisoner coveralls: a single jumpsuit with pockets, a zipper up the center; numbers printed on the back and the right breast. *Prison jumpsuit designs are apparently universal.*

The masked figure looks up and down the corridor, holding up one finger for quiet. "We better go. I didn't go to the trouble of busting you two out just to get zapped by Partherians. More are coming, and they'll be more prepared than these goobers." The stranger turns and walks quickly down the corridor.

"Hey, wait!" the female prisoner shouts. "Where are you going?" She and her companion run after the stranger, following the strange spacesuit around a corner and into a side corridor. Here the deck plating has been lifted up and away, revealing a distinctly fresh burn-hole in the hull. The edges are still faintly red.

The stranger turns to the prisoners. "Lucky the Partherians keep their brig on the lowest decks. Watch the edges here, they're still hot." Without another word, the intruder jumps down the hole.

Hearing shouts from down the corridor, the two prisoners exchange a glance and then follow the stranger into the hole, one after the other.

Partherians aren't known for their intellect, but what they lack in the brains department they make up for in size. Two meters tall and at least a meter wide, their corridors are wide because they are. To most other races, Partherian warships are distinctly ugly. Apparently made with function in mind rather than form, they are angular and blocky, with thickly-armored hulls and weapons everywhere. They resemble a child's toy block, with engines set into one face and weapons mounted on all the rest.

This particular battleship is in deep space, transiting between a Partherian outpost world, and the home system. *Not sure it is good luck or not, that this is the ship tasked with transport, vs a faster courier class ship.*

Landing with a soft thud—thanks to the gravity field around the boarding tube—the intruder steps to one side. "*Ghost*, get ready to go," they say quietly, deactivating their personal shield and smoothly retracting the face shield on their head gear. He is human: somewhere in his thirties, and about six feet tall.

"Working," a sterile male voice replies.

The prisoners land softly next to him. The woman looks at him. "Human?" she says, sounding as shocked as if their savior was a goldfish—if she knew what a goldfish was. While she does know what a human is, they're not exactly commonplace in this sector. Her tall companion looks just as confused.

"Do you want explanations, or do you want to be as far from that Partherian ship as possible?" the human calls over his shoulder, as he heads off, the prisoners hot on his heels. "Our stealth systems will keep them confused for a bit, but the hole in the floor will be a dead give away—more so if we're still at the other end of the hole."

From hidden speakers, the same cool male voice says, "Boarding tube retracting; airlock sealed. Ready to depart."

"Great, thanks!" the stranger says, as the trio arrives at the bridge of the ship. He plops down into the pilot/command station, and begins working the console, "And away we go!"

The ship lurches and tilts to one side as it increases the distance between them and the now fully-alert battleship. The stranger flips a few switches, just before the ship rattles and shakes. "That's weird, they must have gotten some upgraded sensors from someone. Partherian sensors shouldn't be able to lock on to us that well. *Ghost*, deploy weapons and fire aft guns, keep them busy." The ship lurches as the human pilot twists the ship this way and that, avoiding blazing plasma blasts from the Battleship.

"Acknowledged." The sound of hull plating moving and mechanical parts adjusting and shifting can be heard throughout the ship, followed by the tell-tale whine of energy weapons firing and recharging. The ship lurches again.

The prisoners are holding on to the railings. "What's going on? What can we do?" the woman asks. Sparks erupt from a nearby station, and she rushes to it, her training taking over, to check the position and extinguish any fires.

The stranger is whipping the ship back and forth, evading the more powerful weapons fire. "Damn it!" he shouts. "Hold on to something!" He grabs a slide lever and pushes it forward to the stops.

On the main display, the stars that were careening past steady, then stretch out into a flash of light. Their rescuer lets out a whoop and leans back in his chair. "Well," he says, grinning. "That was exciting!"

THE GHOST

Once the ship has stabilized, the stranger/pilot turns to his guests. "Okay, now we can chat. Those big dummies won't be able to track us at FTL, so even if they've got better sensors than I expected, we're clear." He stands up and offers his hand. "I'm Wil—Wil Calder. You're on my ship, the *Ghost*." When neither of the prisoners reach for his hand, he holds his arms out expansively, spinning in a slow circle.

The female prisoner, who has been walking from console to console in the crowded space, now turns. "This is an Ankarran ship." It is less question, and more of a statement.

"You're good." Wil smiles broadly, clearly impressed. "I'd be surprised if you didn't identify it, but yeah, the *Ghost* is an Ankarran raptor, though modified a bit over the years."

Ankarran Raptors are essentially pocket warships: small, fast, and agile and with enough firepower to take on ships many times their size. The Ankarran are master shipbuilders, supplying many different races with warships, science vessels, and even commercial ships. Ships of all classes and sizes are made in the Ankarran ship-yards. They are expensive, so they're usually rare outside of militaries —whether corporate or government-run—and well-funded research outposts. The Raptor spaceframe was popular for a time, since it only required a small crew to operate, but could travel for extended periods of time and cover vast distances between supply stops. For years, the Ankarrans sold to anyone with enough credits to pay their fees, until the GC and the Peacekeepers insisted on a more exclusive agreement.

"And you're Zephyr," Wil says. "No last name because that's what you peacekeepers do. And your big friend here is Maxim—also no last name. You're both Peacekeepers, or were, until recently. Now you're fugitives of the Partherian Hegemony."

Maxim finally speaks up. "We were set up. We're innocent." His voice is as deep as one might expect from a person as big as he is. His stoic appearance matches his tone. Everything that has happened so far, doesn't seem to have phased him.

"He's right, we're innocent. We were framed." Zephyr looks Wil up and down. "Are you really human?"

Shrugging Wil glances at the console behind him. "Honestly, I don't care—and yes, I am."

"Typical bounty hunter scum." Maxim takes a step toward Wil.

"I wouldn't," Wil warns. "One word and *Ghost* will send a few thousand volts through you. Won't kill ya, but you'll wake up with a killer headache."

Raising her hands, Zephyr turns from Maxim to Wil. "What can we tell you to make you believe us? Handing us over to Peacekeeper Command is a death sentence for us both, and I assume you're not going to hand us back to the Partherians. Is there a bounty? How much is it? Maybe we can pay more? Work off the debt or something?" She pauses, before looking at Wil again. "And really, you're human? Since when are humans out here? I didn't even know you had space flight—has the GC lifted the ban?"

Wil stands and walks over to another station. "Bounty? There's no bounty on you, in fact, there's no record of you, other than a news blurb buried in the feeds about two rogue Peacekeepers captured by the Partherians for trafficking in contraband. The Peacekeepers didn't even try to negotiate getting you back. Hate to break it to you, but you've been disavowed. As for your other question, yes, I am a human, flesh and blood—red blood, in case you were gonna ask. As to how I got out here, it's a long story; I'm pretty sure I'm the only one, which suits me just fine. And no, the GC hasn't lifted the ban." He starts flipping switches and adjusting settings. Zephyr assumes he is getting ready to make a call to Peacekeeper Command.

"Look," she says, "whether you believe us or not, or even care, it doesn't matter. We're trying to stop a war. The Peacekeepers are planning to stir up a few regional brush fires to force unaffiliated systems to join GC. We found out and got set up. I'm guessing the Partherians got an anonymous tip that a Peacekeeper shuttle was carrying contraband through their territory and, what do you know, they found us. Our superiors hid something—we were never told what it was we were accused of carrying."

Wil looks up from what he's doing. "Go figure, right? Group calls themselves Peacekeepers, works for the hugest galactic government— you'd think they'd consider it a job well done, with the peace and all, but nope, always looking for more reasons to exist and expand your power base. Y'all are a lot like humans, know that? Remind me to tell you about my bank."

"There's no need to insult us," Maxim says, a sour look on his face. So far he has not moved from where he stopped a minute before: arms crossed, eyes scanning the small space.

He's a big one, Wil thinks.

"What he means, is that greed is universal," Zephyr says, staring hard at Wil. "So if there's no bounty, why did you rescue us from the Partherians?"

Turning away from the display, Wil gestures to the nearest seats and walks back to his pilot station. "Tell me the whole story—we've got a while before we get there."

"Where?" Maxim asks, taking a seat.

Zephyr sits, too, and turns to Wil. "It's not that long a story, but here goes. Maxim and I are... were part of a special operations detail.

Our commander was a Centurion named Janus." At this, Wil makes a face, but Zephyr presses on: "I was working on some signal intercepts from... from non-Peacekeeper sources, when I stumbled across a feed that was Peacekeeper in origin, from the command complex I was in. Somehow it had been collected and bundled in with the intercepts—likely due to its destination. When I opened it, I saw that Janus and several other high-ranking officers in Peacekeeper Command were planning several attacks throughout the frontier... but not attacks by Peacekeepers. They were funding rebel groups to destabilize independent systems, attacks with the goal of creating panic to increase the need for Peacekeeper services, and—more importantly to them—Peacekeeper ships, in these systems. Nearly ten in all—systems, that is. Ten new systems joining the GC would be huge, obviously.

"The data files must have had meta data tracking on them, because no sooner had I read the transcripts than I was summoned to Janus' office." The look on her face is pained.

"I take it you didn't go to his office," Wil interjects, wryly. "How's the big guy here fit in?"

Zephyr looks at Maxim. "No, I didn't. I called Maxim—he's my partner."

"Wait, like work partner? Or you two are bumping uglies?" Wil says, looking more interested than he has for the whole conversation, leaning forward. "This is getting interesting."

"Bumping *what*?! How dare you!" Maxim leaps out of his seat, and before he can remember Wil's earlier warning or take the five steps needed to cross the distance between them, Wil utters an unfamiliar word and a bolt of blue current arcs from the ceiling, cutting through Maxim to the deck plates, and dropping the huge Peacekeeper to the ground.

"Maxim!" Zephyr is out of her seat and at his side in the blink of an eye.

Wil barely even reacts. "Okay then, that answers that. Oh, and he'll be fine—it's a very mild shock, especially for a Peacekeeper. I did warn him; you were there, you heard me. This isn't my fault."

As he speaks, Maxim starts to stir, and Zephyr helps her colleague back to his seat. After a few muttered words—*something, something human*—she turns to Wil. "Yes, he's my lover. I told him what we'd found, and we agreed to flee, to take the information to Tarsis. We were en route when the Partherians attacked us."

Wil looks Zephyr in the eyes. "Cool. I actually don't care, but it's good to know as much about your crew as possible." To say his smile is broad would be an understatement. "*Ghost*, please show our new crew to the crew quarters, one of the larger births."

"Acknowledged," the cool male voice of the ship replies. The door to the bridge opens, and a wall panel lights up. "Please follow the illuminated wall panel."

Helping Maxim out the door, Zephyr turns back to face Wil. "Thank you. Are all humans as... well, weird, as you?"

"You've no idea," he says, already turning back to the pilot console, as the door to the bridge closes behind them.

BREAKFAST

The ship's central crew space is made up of a lounge area, a kitchenette with a table—built into the side of the room—and a few other bits and pieces to make the space somewhat "homey."

"So... where are we going?" Zephyr asks, from across the table. She and Maxim have been holed up in their quarters since the previous night. Their quarters aboard the ship aren't half bad, considering the type of ship it is. Wil had the computer keep an eye on them when he finally went to bed, and when he woke up, they were both in the galley, cooking.

"Good morning to you too," Wil says, punching buttons on a machine. "We're going to Fury..." he holds up his hand as both of their heads snap around to face him, mouths making what would be in other circumstances a comical 'o' shape. "Hey, don't burn that bacon, it's the last until I get more."

"What's bacon?" Maxim asks, before Zephyr makes a signal to cut him off. "Fury is a *hell hole*, even the Peacekeepers don't like to go there," Maxim mutters, going back to shoving the bacon around in the pan.

"He's not wrong," Zephyr says, not taking her eyes off Wil. She is still in her prisoner jumpsuit, just like Maxim, are but at least it looks and smells like they've showered.

"No, he's not," Wil says calmly, still focusing on the machine. "And I completely agree. Unfortunately, that doesn't change anything. We're going to Fury. We're going because you two need new identities and there aren't many better places to do that. You also need gear. I've got some spare this 'n' that, but you'll need your own stuff too. Especially things that need to fit right, and weapons you like to use." The machine he's harassing finally makes some grumpy-sounding beeps and a few *thunks*, before beginning to dispense coffee. "Now we're talking," he sighs.

Sliding bacon onto a plate in the center of the table, Maxim turns to Wil. "We have no money."

Zephyr, who had gotten up, now sits down next to him with a bowl of something Wil doesn't recognize, and starts scooping steaming piles of it onto her and Maxim's plates. *Where'd that come from?* he wonders. She looks over at Wil, eyebrow raised. He nods. *Why not?* She drops a pile of the steaming something on a third plate.

Maxim grabs some bacon, putting it on his plate. "We have no money," he repeats. Then he takes a bite, and his eyebrows shoot up in surprise. "This is delicious!"

Wil smiles. "I know, right? On behalf of all humanity, you're welcome. We don't have much to offer the galactic community, but we do have bacon. As for the money—consider it a loan against future payment, future cuts, whatever. I can't use you if you're easily tracked, still running around in Partherian prisoner jumpsuits." He sniffs the pile of something on his plate and then digs in, shoving a piece of bacon into his mouth with it. "I don't know what this is," he says, "or where you found it in my galley, but it's not bad!" He takes a moment to chew his food, then adds, "There's a few shops I trust down there, and a hacker I know who can get you new wrist comm and idents."

They watch as he shovels a few more bites of the mystery stuff and bacon into his mouth. Then he takes a sip of his coffee and continues, "There's also someone I need to see. We're gonna need some money—it wasn't cheap figuring out where you'd be, plus now outfitting you as well. It's not my first choice for work, but it'll pay well, whatever it is, and as far as things go, I trust the source."

Trust might be a strong word to use, Wil reflects ruefully, but he doesn't have many friends in the sector.

Zephyr grabs another strip of bacon. "This really is quite good. Bacon, you said? What's it made of?"

Wil grins and stifles a laugh. "Ask me another time."

"Humans..." Maxim says, watching the display, before turning to his food.

FURY

Fury is one of those planets that no one wants to be on, but is still somehow overcrowded. A mix of people are to be found there—some are there to prey on others, some have been left behind for various reasons, and some simply don't know any better. Then there are those who fall into none of these categories, who tend to be the most dangerous of all.

Each time he comes to Fury, Wil tries to carry himself like he is part of this fourth group. It mostly works—like walking through a tough neighborhood as a kid, trying to look like you belong, like you are tougher than those around you, hoping that everyone buys it. Or in the very worst cases, just acting like the craziest person around.

Wil has had to do both, on Fury.

The *Ghost* sets down on a landing pad near the outer edge of the spaceport. Even though it is by no means a large ship, its size means that it can't fit closer to the center, where the smaller personal yachts and mini cargo haulers dock. Also, Wil has noticed that its very nature tends to make spaceport controllers want to keep it tucked away from most foot traffic. Warships—even small ones, even sitting on the ground—make folks nervous, so they usually try to keep them out of sight.

As the cargo ramp hits the surface with a soft thud, Wil walks out, followed by Zephyr and Maxim, who've finally changed out of their prisoner jumpsuits. Zephyr has found a pair of maintenance overalls to wear, likely left over from before Wil took ownership of the *Ghost*, and Maxim is trying to make do with some of Wil's clothes. This is barely working, Wil realizes, looking the Peacekeeper over.

"Okay, you two. Take this." He hands them a PADD, or PersonAl Data Device—at least that's what Wil assumes it means. H's never actually asked anyone, but everyone he's ever met knows the name. "It's a map and list of places to go. It also has your allowed budget. And it's tied to the *Ghost* and my wrist comm. Meet me back at the ship in 6 tocks. If you get done early, then when you get to the ship just ask for access—it'll call me, and I can let you back in. I assume this doesn't need saying, but I'm saying it anyway: the flight deck and engineering spaces aren't accessible to you without me around." He looks at them both. "Also, don't do anything to draw attention to yourselves. The Peacekeepers here on Fury would rather not deal with issues, but if anyone has been paying attention to the wanted bulletins, you could end up in trouble. Also, don't get killed."

"And where will you be?" Zephyr asks, already thumbing through the list on the PADD. "Aren't you worried we'll run out on you? Not come back?" She glances up from the list, looking Wil straight in the eyes.

"By all means. I'm still not entirely convinced you're going to be worth all this effort, but I'm curious, and bored, so..." He shrugs. "Oh and also, where would you go? You've only got the funds I gave you, which the PADD will only disperse at the locations assigned, and will lock down if I suspect anything and send it the necessary command. And even if you run out on me, after your shopping spree, where would you go? No ship. No friends. Wanted by the Partherians, and by extension the Peacekeepers. As for where I'll be? None of your business."

"He has a point," Maxim says, before turning and walking away.

Zephyr stares at Wil a moment longer, then follows after the large ex-Peacekeeper.

Wil watches them go, turns to his wrist comm and dials up a comm listing. He whistles a tune, singing under his breath, *"Walk like an Egyptian. Duh duh dih—* Oh! Hi, yeah, is Xarrix there? Tell him it's Wil Calder. Yeah, he'll know me—just do it, jeez! Cool, I'll be there in half a tock." He closes the connection and whistles a little more: *"Blond waitresses take their trays, they spin around, and they cross the floor..."* He chooses a different exit out of the spaceport than the two ex-Peacekeepers took.

It's a fifteen-minute walk from where the *Ghost* is docked to the nearest pedestrian exit. The spaceport is designed like every other spaceport Wil has ever seen: essentially a massive stadium-shaped hangar, with no roof. The structure itself is a mix of government offices and for-rent commercial space—mostly import/export businesses, some tourist companies, and the like. This spaceport is only about five stories tall, but is at least a kilometer in diameter, with several hundred ships spread out around the interior space.

CHAPTER 2

SHOPPING

The two ex-Peacekeepers walk through the crowded streets of the spaceport shopping district. Wil had no clothes to fit either of them on board the *Ghost*, and Maxim is eager to get out of his two-sizes-too-small outfit. The first stop on their list is a clothier. The note attached to the map reads: *Don't get fancy — love, Wil.*

The shop isn't overly impressive, though it has a front door, which itself is quite an accomplishment for Fury. As soon as the two enter, the shopkeeper emerges from the back room. It is a small creature; Zephyr isn't sure exactly what race, but it's definitely bipedal, and has all the right body parts she expects in all the places she expects them—at least as far as she can see.

"Well hello there, travelers, you've come to the right place!" it exclaims, suddenly revealing two sets of arms, all four of which wave emphatically. It looks them both up and down. "Don't we have our work cut out for us! I'm Mordo, owner of this fine establishment, and master clothier!" He points to Zephyr, and then to one of the dressing rooms: "You, in there." Then to Maxim, "You in that one—my you're large! You know there's an extra fee for using so much fabric."

Two hours later, the two leave the shop and a waving Mordo with several bags under each arm, clad in entirely new outfits. Zephyr looks over at Maxim. "This might become difficult if each stop ends with this much merchandise—and clothes are likely the lightest of our purchases." Zephyr is not sure she's ever owned this many clothes, and they have spent less than three-quarters of what Wil assigned to them.

Maxim grunts his agreement. He looks left and right, then lets out an ear-splitting whistle, and a small cargo bot comes trundling towards them. It stops a few paces away and opens a hatch in its cargo area. "Please place items inside the cargo area!" it chirps. "Will this rental be a one-stop fair, or shall I follow you for more shopping?"

The hatch closes, and Maxim moves to place his thumb on the small biometric reader, and stops suddenly, looking at the bot. "Passcode only," he says. "No biometrics, and follow us. There'll be a few stops."

The bot takes a moment, then replies, "That method is less secure. Please verbally accept the updated terms, then provide the passcode."

Maxim sighs. "I accept the updated terms; your passcode is terminus, bravo, nine, one, eight, four, four, delta. End passcode."

"Accepted," the bot replies.

"Follow us." Maxim looks at Zephyr, smiling. She enjoys seeing him like this; it's so rare. He waves both hands at her. "See? Problem solved."

Zephyr checks the PADD, crossing off the first item on the list, clothes, and looks at the next item. Smiling, she holds the PADD up for Maxim to see, he smiles too. "Finally."

They head off in the indicated direction, to find a weapons dealer named Prux.

Prux turns out to be an old and scarred Quilant, who—aside from being an arms dealer—owes Wil a favor or two. The two ex-Peacekeepers are like children in a candy shop. They start in the front of the pistols and grenades, picking things up, holding them, aiming them. Some get put back on the wall; others into a small bin Prux is holding as she follows them around her shop. After the pistols and assorted small arms, they move on to the rifles and, as Maxim puts it, "the fun stuff."

After an hour of happily grabbing weapons, comparing them against others, changing what's in the in the bin and then changing them back again, Prux leads them to a back room. "I have something special," she says, "that I think just might be right for you."

MEETINGS

Wil walks confidently into the bar—at least, he thinks of it as a bar. It kind of looks like a TGI Friday's, except instead of tchotchkes everywhere this place has animal skins, weapons, and various bits of technology he can't readily identify. The crowd is what you'd expect at a shithole bar near a shithole spaceport, on a shithole planet. As such, Wil is armed, with his personal shield charged and ready to activate at only a simple hand gesture.

The place is dark, but it isn't hard to know where Xarrix will be. He's usually in the back, at a booth with the privacy screen active, two guards of unidentifiable race and gender standing ready on either side.

Sure enough, straight back from the door, Wil sees exactly that. He heads to the bar, and makes eye contact with the barkeep. "Gimme a grum." He touches his wrist comm, sending the payment, as the barkeep hands him a glass of something that looks and tastes a lot like beer. Wil has never figured out how grum is made or what it's made from. If he's honest with himself, he doesn't want to know, since real beer is nearly impossible to get without a trip home, and that's not high on his list of things to do anytime soon.

He takes his drink to the back of the bar, in the direction of the booth and the two goons. They watch him coming and don't move until he's right in front of the booth's privacy screen. Then they each take a step towards the middle, creating a wall of goon right in front of him.

"Hi, goons," Wil says, cheerily. "He's expecting me."

One of the goons lifts its wrist comm and whispers into it. Since the thing isn't speaking standard, it could have shouted—Wil wouldn't have understood it any better. A few seconds pass, then something chirps in an earpiece; one goon looks at the other goon, and nods. Without a word, they part, and the privacy screen fades away with a shimmer.

Wil slips into the booth. No sooner has he scooted to the middle of the bench than the privacy screen reactivates with a slight pop-sizzle. He can still see out through the hazy energy barrier, but now no one can see in, he knows.

"Well, well, if it isn't my favorite... what are you again?" The being across the table from Wil, Xarrix, is an Trenbal, and a particularly ugly one at that. Standing about two meters tall, with two arms, two legs, a prehensile tail, and a face like a velociraptor, the Trenbal are a pretty scary race. Most are pacifists; Xarrix is not. Wil had met him shortly after acquiring the *Ghost*, when he needed some funds in his account and he'd been happy to take whatever jobs Xarrix needed doing. Some of them still woke Wil up at night, even now.

Wil took a sip of his grum, never taking his gaze off Xarrix. Arquillians have wide-set eyes, so looking one in the eyes is often impossible. Wil chooses instead to stare at a spot in the center of the crime boss's head.

"I'm human, you ugly lizard." He smiles at the look of incomprehension on Xarrix's face. "You have work?"

Xarrix shakes his head, making a combined hissing and clucking sound, which never fails to freak Wil out. "I didn't think you were taking those types of jobs anymore?"

"Well since I was in this sector, I figured I'd say hello, and check. I'm not looking for anything too out there, but I picked up some crew

—I could use an easy win to get the bank accounts back up to where I'm comfortable."

Xarrix makes a show of consulting his wrist comm, as if he keeps a file called "super sketchy and illegal things to hire out for.txt" on it. Then looks up at Wil.

"Well, you're in luck, my human friend. I do have something not too 'out there', that might be just the right thing for you and that ship of yours."

THE PAST

"Mission control, this is Discovery One, do you read?" Wil Calder, NASA astronaut, is looking at a dead console. "This is not good," he mutters, before repeating his call.

The mission had been going smoothly, with his small experimental spacepod operating within all expected areas. The small revolutionary powerplant was running; the energy field emitters were all properly charged leading up to the experiment, and the navigation settings were locked into the beacon orbiting Jupiter. So what had gone wrong?

The pod is now drifting in empty space. Wil can't see any planets, anywhere, which might mean he was just past Earth or Jupiter... or somewhere in deep space. If he can just get the power plant rebooted—it had scrammed when whatever-it-was had happened—then that'd be a start in figuring out where he was. The navigation system is, in theory, so advanced it can pick out his location just by comparing the visible stars until it finds a familiar constellation. But that has only been tested in limited ways back home, so...

Unfortunately, NASA opted to send a moderately smart but very skilled pilot on this first mission, instead of an engineer or physicist, or astronomer. All of which are skills that would be valuable right about now. "Okay, here we go," Wil mutters to the pod, as he wiggles around in his seat to get access to the small hatch into the reactor compartment. He silently crosses his fingers that he doesn't have to spacewalk. *I hate spacewalks.*

Discovery One was never designed to be worked on in situ, but certain allowances had to be made, given the unknowns. Wil hadn't thought much about it before, but he is happy for those allowances now, wriggling around in the cramped access space behind his seat. He is fussing with a component when something clicks—and *boom*, lights start turning back on.

"Mission control," he says, quickly. "This is Discovery One, transmitting in the blind. I've got the reactor restarted, and am waiting for it to complete its spin-up cycle before I try any other systems." Wil knows this broadcast is likely a waste of time, and possibly air, if he can't get the scrubbers up and running—but it's policy. Apparently, it has helped astronauts in this situation to stay sane longer. Wil has his doubts, but he follows protocols. The console in front of him beeps, then one by one, lights and displays start to wake up. "It's so good to see you all!" Wil says, slapping the console. "I hope you have good news for me!"

Within minutes the entire pod is back online: reactor at 100%; life support at 100%; navigational sensors at 100%; maneuvering thrusters at 100%; FTL field generator, offline. "SHIT!" Wil punches the console with the FTL Field generator controls on it. "Well hell. Mission control, this is Discovery One. All systems have successfully rebooted, except one. The FTL Field generator seems to be offline. I'm going to try and restart it again, see if it's just a software bug. I honestly don't know what I'll do after that."

Two reboots later, and the computer still reports that the highly experimental device, designed to create an energy field around the ship to propel it faster than light, is offline. Over one hundred automated drone tests had gone perfectly: all the way to Jupiter and back. This is only the second manned attempt, and Wil is now adrift somewhere around the orbit of Neptune. *Very* far from Jupiter. He's tried all the diagnostics he can try from inside the pod; it might be space-walk time, to get out and check the exterior of the pod. It's difficult to imagine something is wrong out there—there have been no collisions, and technically the FTL field generator had worked the first time, since it got him here to the outer edge of the solar system. But what else is there to do—sit here and do nothing? Wil knows no rescue is coming.

At least with life support working, he's able to cycle the air out of the cockpit and store it, versus having to lose it, which would mean opening the pod up to space. Unfortunately, that's as far as the good news goes: the pod is fine. All the emitters are where they should be and look undamaged.

"Well, shit." Wil stands on the pod, his magnet boots holding him to its surface. There's nothing to see in any direction but stars.

"There are worse views, that's for sure," he says, debating whether it'd be better to die standing here atop his crippled craft, or go back inside and have a few more days of life with the rations and life support system running. Tough call. He climbs back into the pod and closes the hatch. At least for now, he's not completely without hope. But there's still time to change his mind, of course.

CLEAN SLATES

The last stop on their shopping trip is the one Zephyr has been dreading ever since they left the ship. They're standing in front of what might be considered a storefront—except there's nothing to indicate that it's open for business or ever has been, and a lot to indicate, or at least trying to suggest, that it's presently abandoned. But the address is on Wil's map, so this must be the place. She looks around, then knocks on the door.

After a minute, she knocks again. Still nothing. Looking at the PADD, she sees a note from Wil attached to this entry: *knock three times, then two times, then five times.*

"Oops, did it wrong." She looks up at Maxim, then knocks the pattern in the file. She shrugs.

The door opens a crack. It's dark inside the store. "Who are you?" a high-pitched voice says, from about Maxim's waist level.

"Wil... uh, Maxim, what did he say his last name was? Wait—I remember. Calder, Wil Calder sent us. He's a human, says he knows you."

The door opens wider. "Come in then." A small three-fingered hand waves them in. As soon as the door closes the lights come up, slowly, so it's not too blinding, but Zephyr immediately sees that they're standing in an ante room behind the storefront—one that's apparently well-protected. The fields she can see shimmering are far more powerful-looking than just privacy screens. Behind the door is a small creature, green, about a meter in height, wearing a multi-pocketed jumpsuit with various tools tucked in here and there. Brailack, she thinks their race is called

"So... what do you want?" the creature asks, walking back toward one of the screens, which shimmers as he passes through it. "I'm busy."

The field stays powered down, so Zephyr and Maxim follow, finding themselves in a workshop. Screens and wrist comms are lying everywhere in various states of disassembly. Parts from things Zephyr can't identify cover most of the workbench surfaces. "We need new identities," she says. "New wrist comms. The works."

"You got credits?" The small creature hops up on a stool in front of a bank of monitors. "The works ain't cheap, and there's no bulk discount."

Zephyr accesses the section of the PADD marked for this part of their shopping trip, and sends the funds. "We'll need our records completely wiped, everywhere, even in Peacekeeper datasets."

"You came to the right guy then. I can do it, will take about a tock. You can wait over there." The creature points to what looks like an attempt at making a comfortable lounge. Zephyr catches Maxim grimacing.

One at a time, they are asked over to the bank of consoles and displays, to rest their palm on a reader. They have no idents; the Partherians had taken them.

"Woah, you two are in some deep dren. Wil is certainly hanging around interesting company these days. Partherians and Peacekeepers... Grolack, that's a lot of trouble." The creature looks up from his array of screens. "Wil hooked you up, Ben-Ari is the best!" Zephyr assumes he means himself. "You have wrist comms?" He holds out his tiny green hand.

"No, sorry, we'll need new ones. Wil rescued us from a

Partherian battleship, all we had on us was the jumpsuits they put us in. The funds we just transferred should be sufficient." When the small being looks like he's about to start negotiating, Maxim does his best menacing growl.

"Fine, fine! Go pick out what you want from the Fabricator!" Ben-Ari waves his hand towards the opposite corner of the room.

The Fabricator is an older model, but is still loaded with plenty of designs. Maxim picks out one that is as close to a military design as he can get, all angles and bulkiness. He places his arm in the scanning area, and watches as a beam of light passes up and down his forearm. Zephyr selects a more sleek design, contoured to her forearm, lets her arm get scanned.

From across the room, Ben-Ari says only, "Excellent choices." Then he gets back to work.

CHAPTER 3

TIME TO GO

Ben-Ari is working at his terminals muttering to himself. Maxim and Zephyr are sitting in the "customer lounge", watching an episodic vid-drama set on a space station. Suddenly the diminutive alien jumps from his stool, knocking over a piece of equipment that neither ex-Peacekeeper recognizes.

"Were you two followed?!" he shrieks. He taps on his wrist comm and energy fields spring to life around the front entry area.

Maxim and Zephyr look at each other. "No, and we didn't even leave our cargo bot outside—we sent it to the spaceport to wait. Why?" Both are standing now, looking tense.

Ben-Ari runs back to his primary workstation and tosses them each a wrist comm. "These are done. We have company, someone musta spotted you!" He waves his hand in a gesture that must have been a trigger motion, as several screens light up suddenly, showing external views of the storefront. At least a dozen Peacekeepers are standing in the street outside the front door. One of them is holding what looks like a doorbuster, a device designed to hack into any door's security protocols, and failing that, to generate a explosion to blow said door in.

Maxim and Zephyr both draw their newly-acquired sidearms,

looking around for defensible positions. There's no shortage of junk in the space, but none of it seems like it'll stop a blaster bolt, and certainly not a dozen or two of them.

"Good luck!" Ben-Ari screams from a doorway that neither ex-Peacekeeper could say was there a moment ago. It is already starting to close after him.

"Wait!" Zephyr calls, racing toward the closing door. She reaches it just in time to jam her pulse pistol into the gap. "Come on, Maxim!"

He rushes over, and they both pry the door open just enough to slip through. The door clicks closed behind them, and up ahead they see the small Brailack trundling along a secret hallway.

Ben-Ari groans loud enough that they can hear, then shouts over his shoulder, "Come on then! You better not slow me down, or get me noticed and killed!" Somewhere along the way, the small green-skinned being has grabbed a scaled-down energy rifle. Maxim decides to ask about that later. They're in a hallway, running along the back wall of the store, which reaches well past where the store ended. Does this hallway go into the shop next door? What is next door? Maxim can't recall. He's getting sloppy; he can't remember whether it was open or closed, or just an abandoned shop. He'd never have made that mistake a cycle ago, when he was a Peacekeeper. Lives depended on knowing these things.

They've barely run five meters when the building shakes. Through the wall they can hear shouting. The breach team is following Peacekeeper protocol: announcing themselves loudly while stunner grenades explode all around. The sound of failing energy shields can clearly be heard too—it is doubtful Ben-Ari that expected his defenses to come up against Peacekeepers. Is this hallway shielded? If not, the Peacekeepers will pick up their body heat in seconds.

Seeming to sense Maxim's thoughts, Ben-Ari calls back, "Don't worry, I've reinforced this hallway. We should be clear for at least another few ticks. Then you two are on your own—I don't want you dragging me down, or getting me shot."

Maxim growls under his breath.

Without warning, Ben-Ari breaks left through a hatchway that's barely visible in the wall. Suddenly they're in the alley behind the shops, about four stalls down. There's trash on both sides of the door, and Zephyr realizes that this is intentional. Behind the piles, they're clear of the secret hallway, and able to look up and down the alley without being seen by anyone else in the alley—a good thing, because six Peacekeepers are standing around the back door of the store Ben-Ari recently called home.

"Okay, bye," the creature whispers to them, before heading off in the opposite direction.

Maxim isn't even sure he knows the name of the spaceport or the city that surrounds it, but he assumes it's a common name, to match the nondescript nature of the place. All that's visible is run-down buildings, shops, and residences. Nothing looks new. Certainly, nothing shines, as it's all uniformly covered with a layer of grime, which he can only hope is just dirt.

"You know they know who you are, right?" Zephyr whispers after the retreating hacker. "You're not safe either. Help us get to the spaceport, and we can keep you safe. Wil will keep you safe."

Ben-Ari stops, and stands there a few seconds, considering. Then he turns his head. "Fine, come on." He continues on, this time at a run.

The three are soon running as fast and as quiet as they can, the small green-skinned hacker in the lead, winding this way and that through what feels like progressively more disgusting alleyways.

"Where are we going?" Maxim whispers. Luckily, his Peace-keeper training means that even as fast as Ben-Ari is running, it's no more than a fast walk for Maxim. "The spaceport isn't in this direction."

"I know that! You think I don't know that? I've lived in this piece of crap joint for the last five cycles. You think I don't know where the spaceport is?!" Ben-Ari screech-whispers, without turning his head. "I have a cache a few blocks from here. We'll stop there, then head to your ship."

As far as the two ex-Peacekeepers can tell they're not being pursued. There's no indication they were seen leaving Ben-Ari's workshop. Knowing what to look and listen for, both are as certain as they can be that no drones are following them. It isn't a 100% certainty, but it is the best they can manage. Peacekeeper drones are meant to be quiet, but not silent, which is a good thing. Peacekeepers don't launch drones unless they need too, so it's possible they aren't taking this issue seriously, given the location.

Ben-Ari comes to a stop, brushing dirt and grime off a control pad next to a door that looks nearly rusted shut. He punches in a code and with a louder-than-ideal groan the door slides inward. Squeezing through the gap, the little hacker whispers back, "Come on, push that closed when you get in."

When Zephyr and Maxim enter the small space beyond, they find themselves speechless. No more than 3 meters wide in each direction, the room is packed with shelves, and piles of equipment and weapons. Ben-Ari is running from rack to rack—climbing, grabbing, tossing. He's swapping out things he had in his pockets for new things, none of which Maxim or Zephyr recognize. The pockets of his jumpsuit are beginning to bulge, and there's a large pack in the middle of the room, nearly full. "I just need another minute," he pants.

"What's the rush?" Maxim asks, just as the lighting shifts from harsh white to red. A speaker hidden somewhere in the room emits three sharp beeps then goes silent. "What was that?" Maxim and Zephyr are looking all around the chamber.

"That, you big jinx, means they're here. Well not 'here' here, but on this block. Someone tripped one of my early warning sensors—they're placed around the ends of the alley." Ben-Ari climbs down one set of shelves, drops something in the pack, and is immediately up another set of shelves rummaging around for something else.

"They must have had a drone or two in the area and it spotted us leaving. The alarm means they're in the alleyway we just came from."

"How are we going to get out of here? Is there another exit?" Zephyr asks, looking around the room, not seeing any other door or hallway, other than the one they've come from. It's not an ideal space for a last stand, but at least the doorway is a natural chokepoint.

Dropping back to the ground and slipping another unidentifiable piece of tech into the pack, Ben-Ari closes the pack and looks at the ex-Peacekeepers. "I hope your sense of smell isn't very strong." He hefts the bag, and shoves some things aside to reveal a grate in the floor.

"Oh no," whispers Zephyr. "Please no."

THE TEAM GROWS, MORE

Wil is walking back through one of the food vendor alleys when he sees a troop of Peacekeepers crossing at the next intersection, heading for—among other things—the shopping district. It could be anything. Peacekeepers aren't exactly commonplace on Fury, but seeing them isn't unheard of. Even on a planet like Fury, if the criminal is valuable enough, the Peacekeepers will show up.

"Oh shit," Wil mutters. As casually as he can, he whispers into his wrist comm, "*Ghost*, begin pre-flight procedures." He drops his arm back down without even waiting for the voice of the ship to confirm his order.

Wil turns down a street that will take him more directly to the spaceport. If his two new crew members are in trouble, they need to figure it out on their own. If they can get to the *Ghost*, he can get them off planet, but there isn't much he can do against a full squad of armed Peacekeepers, especially when there is likely far more than one squad. If word got around about his new crew members, they're screwed.

"Shit, shit, shit," he mutters, as he winds his way through the crowd and the stalls hawking all manner of food—or things that might be food. He has his sidearm but a fat lot of good it'd do him in this scenario. As he crosses from the city into the spaceport proper, he sees two large Peacekeeper troop transports sitting on the tarmac.

"Shit, shit, shit," he mutters, as he walks as fast as he can, trying to look as inconspicuous as he can. Each transport holds two squads, so there are at least four full Peacekeeper squads in the area. The downside of being the only human in the sector—at least as far as Wil knows—is that you stand out in a crowd. Plenty of races look a lot like humans. Peacekeepers, for example, look pretty close, except for the spots, and the entirely different internal arrangement of organs, and the cranial ridges where their hair should be. Ankarrans are similar too, except for the blueish tint to their skin, and the dexterous tail. A few others look similar—but no one seems to be an exact match, and so a human walking fast across the spaceport isn't that easy to ignore.

"Hey! You there! Stop!" an amplified voice rings out.

"Shit," Wil mutters again, and slows down. He concentrates on looking as innocent as he can. "Who? Me?" he says, slowly raising his hands away from his side, the universal gesture for *don't shoot me.*

"Where are you going?" A Peacekeeper walks up to Wil, rifle at their side. With the face shield down Wil can't tell one trooper from another, which is likely done on purpose. Faceless armies are more terrifying, after all. "What's your business here? Show me your ident, please."

"Oh, uh. Me? I'm just going to my ship, officer. Did I do something wrong?" Wil tries to look sheepish, as he transmits his ident from his wrist comm. Well, it's *an* ident—one of many Wil has purchased over the years. This one is for a small-time cargo hauler who's barely making the payments on his cargo ship. Hopefully, the trooper won't be too nosey, since there's no actual ship here at the spaceport that would match the record in the ident. Wil is now rethinking his previous frugality when it comes to buying fake idents.

"What kind of name is Han Solo?" The opaque face shield moves from the PADD the trooper is holding to Wil's face.

"Well, I certainly didn't just make it up. Is there a problem here?" They seem to be just harassing people at random, so Wil decides to play the umbrage card—see if he can't speed things along. "Look, no offense, officer, but every fraction of a tock I spend with you, I'm not billing." He's tapping his foot now, doing his best to casually keep his long coat over his pistol. A weapon on Fury isn't illegal, and it'd be more suspicious to be unarmed, but there's no reason to give this trooper any reason to start asking more questions or to dig deeper into Wil's identity.

The trooper holds up their PADD so Wil can see it. "Seen either of these two? They're considered armed and dangerous."

Well, at least Wil knows for sure now why the Peacekeepers are on Fury. Someone must have spotted them on their shopping trip, because right there in living color, using what's likely the prisoner intake photos from the Partherians, are Maxim and Zephyr.

"Nope. Never seen 'em. They're Palorians? Didn't know you guys ever went rogue, or whatever," Wil tuts as the trooper lowers the PADD.

"No one is perfect. They were last seen in the shopping district beyond this spaceport, so be careful—and if you see anything, call it in. Don't engage them."

"Sure thing, I'll do that. That all?" Toe still tapping, one hand on his hip, Wil is looking as put out as he possibly can.

"That's it. Carry on, citizen." The trooper turns to walk away, and Wil spins on his heel to head toward the back of the spaceport. It's going to be tricky, if not impossible, for Zephyr and Maxim to get to the *Ghost*.

"Well, shit. All that money down the drain." He shakes his head. "Now I gotta start looking for new sidekicks all over again. Fuck."

EVERYONE'S HERE

"I might have to have my nose surgically removed after this," Zephyr says, her voice sounding nasal as her fingers pinch her nose. "This is disgusting."

"You two can't turn your sense of smell off? That sucks—makes this much easier. Maybe try breathing through your mouth?" Ben-Ari suggests from the front of their little group, as they trudge through the sewers under the spaceport. "You sure you know where this ship is? Once we pop back up to the surface, I doubt we'll have more than a few fractions of a tock before a drone or some sharp-eyed trooper spots us. I'm still not sure being with you two is really the safest bet, but running around a spaceport is definitely a bad idea."

"If your map of the facility is accurate, the ship is where we pointed," Maxim says, doing his best to breathe only through his mouth, but somehow still smelling the foul mix of—well, he doesn't know what, and doesn't want to—and also somehow tasting it. As it is, he's convinced they'll be burning their boots and possibly their pants the moment they get to the *Ghost*. Such a waste of brand new clothes.

A few minutes later, they come to a halt. The faint light from above is filtering down into the drain from a metal grate overhead. Ben-Ari looks around, and then back down at the PADD he's holding. "Okay, I think this is as close as we're gonna get to Wil's ship. Big man, you hoist me up—I'll take a quick look around before we make a break for it."

"And if you don't see his ship?" Zephyr asks.

"Then we're well and truly grolacked," the little being says, for the first time sounding as deadly serious as the situation warrants. "There are plenty of other grates, but I somehow doubt your ride is going to wait around forever for you to return—especially if he's picked up on the Peacekeeper presence. I can't imagine he likes you that much."

Maxim lifts Ben-Ari up over his head, and they hear the scraping of metal as the small hacker lifts the grate and looks around. "You said it was an Ankarran Raptor, right?" he whispers down.

"Yes," Maxim answers, as a small foot kicks him in the face. "I'll never be clean again," he mutters, spitting something onto the ground.

"Then it's right there. Good job on the location, you two. It's maybe a hundred meters away. Smart to park this far out—I don't see any troopers, and drones would be a flight hazard. Okay, ready?" He looks down at Maxim under his feet and Zephyr next to him. Both nod.

Ben-Ari slides the metal grate aside, and leaps off Maxim's shoulders. He doesn't reappear.

"That little slime weasel!" Zephyr hisses, as she climbs up Maxim's back and out of the hole. Seconds later, she leans down, bracing herself to help the much larger man climb up out of the sewer. About halfway to the *Ghost*, a tiny green being with a huge backpack is trotting as fast as his little legs will carry him.

Maxim climbs up and out of the opening, and slides the grate back into place. The two take off at a run for the relative safety of the *Ghost*. As they overtake Ben-Ari, they lift him and his huge pack up off the ground. Zephyr takes the bag, while Maxim takes the wriggling and screeching Ben-Ari. "Don't make me drop you," Maxim hisses, and the little hacker goes quiet.

As they approach the *Ghost*, Zephyr sees Wil sitting in a chair at the top of the cargo ramp, reading something on a PADD. He puts the PADD down on his lap and looks up at their approach, slowly raising a blaster pistol. "You know, I didn't think I'd see you two again. I'm pretty impressed. Oh, hey, Bennie," he waves, as they stop at the foot of the ramp. "Why'd you bring him with you?" He points the pistol at Ben-Ari.

Ben-Ari wriggles free of Maxim's grip as they enter the cargo area, dropping with a thud. "You burned me, you krebnack! Peace-keepers stormed my workshop, then followed us to one of my caches! I can't stay here now!" He stomps off up into the crew compartment of the ship, shouting back, "Oh, and I saved them! You're welcome!"

Wil looks at Zephyr and Maxim. "Three things. First, unlock your bot, and I'll get it unloaded, since you can't be seen." He points to where the dutiful little cargo bot is sitting near the edge of the *Ghost*'s cargo ramp. Maxim hadn't even noticed it there in their haste to get on board. "Then take those clothes off, toss 'em out on the tarmac, and go shower." He throws them some coveralls, much like the ones Zephyr had worn into the shopping district.

Maxim walks back down toward the bot, reciting his authorization code, and begins stripping out of his utterly disgusting brand-new outfit. "I liked these boots," he mutters as he tosses them, grime-encrusted, out of the hold.

THE PAST

Wil has been sitting in his crippled space pod for a day, transmitting his automated distress call, watching the on-board diagnostics fail— then fail again, then again. He's debating his next steps: stay here adrift for another, what, two days, based on his supply levels? Or sit on the hull until his suit air runs out?

Or there's always the small pill in a pouch on the chestplate of his suit. A pill every astronaut, ever, has taken with them on their missions; a pill none have ever had to use. *Not exactly the first I was hoping for.*

He's reaching for the pill when a blinding light fills the small cockpit. "What the..?!" He can't see anything but the light. He's looking all over, trying to understand what's happening, as the light gets closer and closer, until he finally sees the edges of it, lowering down over his craft... or is he rising? It's hard to tell in space, with no other objects relative to him.

As the light fades, he feels his pod settle on... something. He looks around, and sees he's in some type of ship—that much is obvious. *It must be a cargo hold or shuttle bay or something.* There are no other vessels around, and it's not that large a space, so he decides it's a cargo hold. Why is he in it?

He seals his suit—who knows what the atmosphere is out there? Neither his suit or the pod were designed to look for breathable atmosphere, let alone test it. Then he pops the hatch on the cockpit and crawls out. *Damn this flight suit,* he thinks. No external speakers or mic, so he can't talk to anyone he does find without opening the visor, so if they breathe methane, he's definitely toast. *Shit.* He can't see anyone. Maybe the ship is automated.

Then he feels the deck plates rumble a little and can feel footsteps. He spins around and sees three... aliens, standing in front of him. Two have weapons pointed at him; the other looks unarmed, but is wearing a long coat and some kind of spacesuit under it. None of them have masks on, or any type of breathing equipment, but they're all very clearly different species. *So they all breathe the same atmosphere.* While Wil looks at the trio, a fourth alien appears and walks over to his pod. It crawls up into the cockpit, and connects a hand terminal to it. *Aliens use Thunderbolt?*

Wil looks at the three in front of him, then the alien crawling around his pod, and back to the three. They're talking—he can see their lips moving—but his suit isn't set up for audio once sealed, so he can only hear muffled sounds. He's trembling, standing in front of four aliens, two of which are armed and pointing their weapons at him. The one he assumes is the leader waves to get his attention. He, she, it? Wil isn't sure but assumes the alien is male. It makes a gesture that looks like he wants Wil to remove his helmet.

"Well, I was about to commit suicide, so I guess if they breathe methane the end result is the same," he says to himself, as he unseals the helmet and lifts it up off his head.

"Hi there," the lead alien says. "I'm Lanksham, the captain of this ship. And you are?"

"Uh. Hi." Wil blinks a few dozen times. "I'm uh..."

"Think it's damaged?" one of the armed aliens asks Lanksham, who elbows it in the side and makes a growling sound.

"I'm uh. Wil, Wil Calder, from Denver. Denver Colorado... in uh, America, the United States of America... uh, on planet Earth," Wil stammers. *They speak English?!*

"Okay, well hello Wil Calder from Den-var Cah lore addo, planet Earth. As I said, I'm Lanksham, this is my ship the *Reaper*, and we picked up your beacon." He looks over at the smaller alien still pawing at Wil's craft. "Anything we can use or sell?"

The small alien pops up out of the cockpit and waggles one hand. Apparently, this is the universal gesture for *not really*. "Not a lot, pretty primitive stuff. Surprised this one lived—looks like maybe a first attempt at FTL?"

It looks at Wil, who nods. "Second, actually."

"Yeah, nothing here we can use, but we can probably strip it down for materials to melt down."

Wil turns at that. "Hey, that's my ship you're talking about!" He starts to move toward the craft, and the two aliens surrounding Lanksham snap their weapons up, stopping Wil dead in his tracks.

"Actually, it's my ship, such as it is. It's salvage." Lanksham's voice is calm. "Technically, of course, you have to be dead for it to be salvage, so take care what your next words or actions are. They could be the difference between us taking you with us, or us leaving you here."

Lanksham is a little over two meters tall. His skin has a bluish tint, and his eyes are larger than humans, and are a bright, startling yellow. Otherwise, though, he's remarkably human-like: he has four fingers and a thumb on each of his two hands on his two arms, and a head about the size of a humans'. There's no lanky, skinny body and oversized head, like in the abduction movies. He's got white hair, too. The other three in the room are all sort of similar. The small one is a bit more alien-abduction-movie looking: bigger head, little body, frail-looking limbs. It seems like this one has three fingers, not five, and he's only a meter or so tall. Okay, Wil decides, the other two aren't *that* similar. They're a little taller than him, and muscled; one is red and the other a milky white. The red one has small horns running upwards from its nose, right over its bald head, while the white one has greenish hair done up in a top knot on its mostly shaved head. *Yeah, not similar at all.*

Wil looks the alien captain in the eyes. "Oh, uh, okay, yeah. Sorry." *Sorry NASA, don't think you're gonna get your spacecraft back. Hope it's insured. For that matter, am I insured?*

CHAPTER 4

UNDERWAY

Leaving Fury was easier than Wil had expected, largely thanks to an indignant hacker named Ben-Ari.

"You know, you're pretty damn handy to have around Bennie," Wil snickers. "Maybe you can stay if you're always this useful." Bennie turns and scowls at him from one of the stations on the small bridge. He's only been on the ship an hour, but the station has already been disassembled and rebuilt to suit the diminutive Brailack's needs.

"It's your fault I'm here, you idiot. I had a good thing going down there, and you and your goon squad screwed it up." Bennie swivels around in his chair. "Why would I want to work with you, anyway?"

While Bennie was ranting, Zephyr and Maxim have arrived onto the bridge. "We saw your place, this, such as it is, is an improvement." Zephyr spreads her hands expansively.

Bennie glowers at her. "It was my own place. I had clients that paid well. Those caches don't come pre-stocked, you know? It cost a fortune to set up and secure each one. Plus, what about my clients? They depend on me."

Zephyr looks him in the eye. "They depend on you for illegal hacking. I'm sure they'll find another hacker."

Growling and jumping off his chair, Bennie storms off the bridge. "Whatever!"

Maxim turns to Wil. "What's his problem? This ship needs some work, but it's not even a competition. His workshop was a pile of crap."

Wil walks over to one of the auxiliary stations and inputs some commands into it. A Peacekeeper intel file appears on the screen: Ben-Ari's. "You'll get used to Bennie. He's a Brailack—they're all like that, acerbic little assholes. But they're amazing with technology, like *crazy* amazing, like Tony Stark amazing. Rumor has it they've all got tech embedded into their brains at birth, to help them operate computers faster. Something about near-field communication, or something. So we'll live with him." The file vanishes, to be replaced with the default view of the star field at FTL. "We've got a few days travel time ahead of us. You two might as well go get all your stuff sorted out and put away."

Zephyr leans over to Maxim. "Who's Tony Stark?"

"Your guess is as good as mine."

As they walk to the hatch leading out of the bridge, Zephyr turns around. "We'll be in the cargo hold, if you need us."

Wil waves one hand, distractedly.

Walking down the main corridor of the ship, Maxim lets out a low whistle. "Who'd have guessed this is where we'd end up?"

Zephyr looks up at him, then gets on her tip-toes and plants a light kiss on his cheek. "At least we're together. And yeah, I thought we'd die in a Partherian labor camp, but now here we are, adopted crew on a warship owned by a crazy human, of all things. Strange times for sure."

They cross through the main crew lounge, stopping in front of the hatch that leads to the upper section of the cargo hold. "What should we do about the GC and the Peacekeepers? They're still plotting to take over some of the unaffiliated systems."

Zephyr opens the hatch, letting Maxim through. "I don't know. We'll have to try and convince Wil to do something. What that something *is* though, I don't know. What can two ex-Peacekeepers, a Brailack, and a human, of all things, hope to do against the GC?"

The big Palorian nods. "Do humans have any super powers?" As they take the stairs to the main cargo hold deck, he adds, "It would definitely seem like we have no options. No one would believe us if we went public, especially after escaping Partherian custody and being disavowed by the Peacekeepers."

They reach the pile of stuff they had bought: bags and boxes of clothing and equipment, also weapons. Zephyr pulls a pulse rifle out of a box, examining it. "You know, this is almost as good as the one I had in the service—who'd've guessed."

Maxim looks at her and her weapon. Then he pulls a large multi-barreled weapon out of its box. "I can't wait to use this," he grins.

Putting down her rifle, Zephyr walks over to a corner of the hold and grabs a hover sled. "Here, let's put all the weapons and tech on this, and take it to the staging room." They quickly load the sled, then just as quickly leave for their quarters.

Thirty minutes later, looking a little disheveled, the two Palorians come back to the hold and guide their grav sled through the ship back to the staging room-cum-armory that sits between the two airlocks on the forward section of the ship.

Looking at one particular box, Zephyr nudges Maxim. "He's really going to freak when he sees what's in there."

Maxim nods. "I can't wait."

UPGRADES

The engineering space of the *Ghost* isn't somewhere Wil visits often. Not only is this a testament to the engineering prowess of the Ankarran shipyards, but also to how little knowledge he has about most of the stuff in there. Whenever the computer had indicated a problem, he'd simply paid to have a trustworthy shipyard work on the problem.

This isn't the most cost-effective solution, but Wil hasn't yet met an engineer yet he's liked enough to let live on his ship. As it is, the sudden addition of three new crew members is having unexpected side effects. For starters, his habit of walking around in his boxers had to come to a screeching halt the day Bennie saw him and fell into an uncontrollable fit of laughter for nearly ten minutes.

But Wil's in the engineering space now, looking around while listening to Bennie prattle on about something he'd done to the computer to improve the efficiency of something, the details lost in the noise coming from the computer access crawlspace. The main processor core is also located in the engineering area, making it almost impossible to hear anything.

"You did what?" Wil kneels down and shouts, then falls back with a yelp as a small green face is suddenly an inch from his.

"I said," and Bennie crawls out of the access, and replaces the cover, "that I was able to adjust some of the learning protocols, as well as some of the... are you listening?" Wil is standing there, his eyes not focused on anything, certainly not focused on Bennie and his explanation.

"What? Oh, sorry, no. No, I wasn't. Gimme the short version, please." Wil hands Bennie a power tool, to secure the access cover.

"The computer can react faster to what's happening now; it'll learn faster from experience, and is a tad more sentient." Bennie has been in the engineering space for hours—Wil's not sure if that's good or bad.

"Oh, okay then. Was that what you wanted to talk to me about? Nice work, by the way." Wil starts moving toward the hatchway.

"Well, no. I coulda sent you a report on these upgrades, or just not told you, since I doubt you'd have caught on anyway. I wanted to inform you that if I'm gonna be here on the ship, we should get a few things straight. Namely my role, my pay, and—more importantly—my shopping list. The computer lab, if that's what you'd call it—which I wouldn't—is so weak. Are those computers from your planet or something? I've seen more power in kid's toys."

Bennie begins to tidy up some tools that Wil has never seen but clearly belong here, since Bennie puts them away in a drawer. The engineering space isn't huge—or at least the part of it that's supposed to be occupied by people. There's a main engineering systems diagram against one wall, a multi-function table-cum-work area in the middle of the room, and two identical configurable workstations over by the engine.

The engine itself is a massive—well, good-sized—reactor mounted at the back of the chamber. Wil is thankful that the entire system is largely automated. When he took control of the ship, he'd have been screwed if he had to know how the engine worked. Since then, he's picked up the fundamental theories, but that's about it. Having Bennie around might be more of a blessing than not—assuming Wil doesn't end up spacing him in frustration.

"Like I said after we broke orbit, you're welcome to hang out here. I think having someone with your skills might be a huge win for us. As far as anything else goes, there aren't much in the way of roles here. It's my ship, my rules, and you and the Palorians are crew. If that's not okay, then after we're done, I'll drop ya off anywhere ya like, so long as I'm already going there.

"And as for pay... well, here's the offer the other two are getting, take it or leave it: fifteen percent of whatever we make from any job we do." Wil holds up a hand when Bennies' mouth opens wider than Wil would have thought possible for a Brailack. "The ship account gets thirty-five percent, and I get twenty percent. That's how it works. Close your maw, your teeth are freaking me out. Again—you can take it or leave it."

Bennie closes his mouth, and Wil can see him thinking it over. Then, slowly, he nods. "Good. Last thing, your shopping list—lemme see it. If you're gonna be here and be useful, I understand you need gear, and we'll get what we can. No promises on everything, but we'll see. Fair?" Wil stands up and heads over to the hatch, slowing just enough to let Bennie answer.

"Fine, that sounds fair."

"Then welcome to my crew!" Wil shouts, as he exits engineering into the main crew space.

SETTLING IN

When Wil walks out of Engineering, Maxim is sitting in the crew area with a fully disassembled pulse rifle on the coffee table.

"Having fun with your new toys?" Wil asks.

Maxim doesn't look up from his task. "Yes. It feels good to have equipment to work on. Thank you," he adds.

"Don't mention it." Wil falls into a seat opposite the big ex-Peace-keeper. "Where's your girlfriend?"

The big Palorian finally looks up from his task, making a low kind of growling sound. "Zephyr is on the bridge." He looks back down at the rifle.

Wil looks up at the ceiling. "Computer, please have Zephyr and Bennie join us in the lounge."

"Sure thing, captain," comes the reply. It's the same voice Wil had heard since he first got the *Ghost*, but now it has... personality?

"Um, what's that now?" Wil is looking around.

Maxim looks up and shrugs. "That's new."

"Computer, are you working properly?"

"I am functioning at 100% efficiency. All ship systems are normal. Why do you ask?"

This is getting weird, thinks Wil.

At that moment, Bennie comes in from the engineering space. "Pretty cool, huh? Like I was telling you before, I upgraded the learning algorithms and sentience protocols."

"You... told me about this?" Wil looks at Maxim, who's still looking at him, and who shrugs, again, before looking back down at the rifle.

Bennie sighs and drops his tiny frame into the chair next to Wil. "Yes. Yes. I told you about this, then you got this goofy... well, goofier than normal, look on your face, and kinda zoned out. Then I think you then changed the subject. Sir." Bennie gives a fist-pounding salute of some sort, or at least Wil assumes that's what it's supposed to be.

"Okay, one? Never do that, whatever that is, again—jeez dude, you look like a green Nazi. Two, do you mean the computer's smarter? More interactive?" Wil is leaning forward, interested. "Like, is the ship *alive* now?"

Bennie almost falls out of the chair from the convulsions he's suffering, laughing as hard as he is. "Oh, gods. I can't breathe. 'Is it alive?' Yes, you dumb... what are you again? Whatever, doesn't matter. No, it isn't alive. It's just slightly more interactive now, has a rudimentary intelligence."

"Oh. Well, that's good I guess. Kind of a let down, but whatever. Cool." Wil is a bit red. He mumbles, "I was going to call it Jarvis."

"What's all the laughing about?" Zephyr asks, coming in from the corridor connecting the bridge to the main body of the ship. She pushes Maxim over and slides in beside him at the kitchen table. Then she pulls out her own pulse pistol and starts to break it down.

Bennie, in between deep breaths, wheezes, "Wil thought I made the ship's computer into an AI."

She looks from Bennie to Wil. "Really?"

Wil just shrugs. "Okay, look, whatever, the ship isn't a super cool, super smart AI, it's just a little more personable. That's fine, whatever. Moving on." He walks over to a wall-mounted display, and brings up an admittedly crude drawing of the team. He hits a button, and it comes to life. He starts narrating: "This is us. I've told Bennie this, but wanted you two to hear it too." On screen, the animated crew goes through some kind of heist, robbing oddly-drawn aliens with tails and long teeth, then dancing around with bags in each hand.

"What the hell is that? What's in the bags?" Maxim is leaning forward over the table, watching the movie. "Is that supposed to be me?"

Wil pushes another button. Now the animated crew is walking up the cargo ramp, depositing their bags in the hold next to a little piggy bank, the counter going up in increments with each bag dropped.

"I'm so lost," Bennie says, looking from the display to Wil, then the ex-Peacekeepers. "Are we feeding that big pink monster the money we just stole?"

Zephyr looks at the Brailack hacker. "Money? Is that what's in those bags? What's that symbol mean? That's money? What's the pink thing?"

Wil shuts off the display, letting out an exasperated sigh. "Fine, I'll explain it the old-fashioned way."

THE PAST

The Galactic Commonwealth has been around for a few hundred years. Someone likely knows exactly how long, but the galaxy is comprised of two groups; those employed by the Galactic Common-wealth, and those who do their best to never think of the GC and do everything they can to avoid it. Technically there's also a third group: those who resist the GC, remaining independent. But this group gets smaller every year.

The GC is made up of dues-paying star systems, spanning right across the sector. Dues are mainly used to fund trade programs, pay the Peacekeepers to police the sector, and other things along those lines—typical government concerns, only on a galactic scale.

The planet Tarsis is the home of the GC; rich and opulent, or proud and snooty, depending on who you ask. Tarsis has spent hundreds of years being the center of the sector, the shining light of justice, government, and—to some—society. Where the Palorians are robust and aggressive, the perfect species for galactic cops, the Tarsi are the perfect bureaucrats. They're only a meter tall, Olive colored, and stand on four legs with antennae protruding from their bald heads. They're preternaturally calm at all times, and love to argue. Their size has usually—at least until the last few hundred years—

made them the victims of other, larger, species. As a result, they rarely leave Tarsis, preferring to exert their considerable power over the rest of the sector via their police force and army, the Peacekeepers. Why leave your comfy, luxurious world, after all, when you have the strongest army in all of space at your disposal?

For most, the GC is just an annoyance which takes some of their taxes; they'll never visit Tarsis, and never (if they're lucky) have a run-in with the Peacekeepers. They'll live and die on their worlds, or in their ships, no more than a blip to the GC. The GC is just a part of life.

Unless, that is, you're one of the free systems. Systems with enough money, power, and allies not to need what the GC has to offer. Fewer and fewer systems like this exist. The GC—while espousing peace and goodwill among all—hates these gaps in its influence. While there are worlds like Fury, which the GC doesn't want to waste the resources needed to rule them, there are other more attractive worlds and systems that the Tarsi want nothing more than to control.

Possibly the only benefit that everyone agrees the GC can offer is their protection of underdeveloped planets. Long ago, the GC realized that races who haven't yet left their planet's orbit—let alone their star system—are at significant risk of exploitation, easily preyed on by pirates, slavers, and conmen. After a few races were wiped out in this way and their planets looted, the GC realized that it had to step in. Now, when new races are discovered, their entire star system is put under protected status. That status is enforced by the Peacekeepers, who randomly patrol protected systems. Their protection is strongest around the orbits of any inhabited planets, but extends to the system as a whole.

Vessels caught within protected systems are shown no mercy. If they fight, they are destroyed; if they surrender, their ships are impounded and their crews imprisoned. No mercy, no exceptions—this is the only way the GC has found to protect these burgeoning systems and their delicate populations. Other punishments the GC had tried were sometimes deemed worth the risk, as the potential payoff could be huge.

Earth was discovered by a scientific exploration team chasing a comet. They picked up radio transmissions and followed them to the source. This was in the mid-1960s, when Earth was first putting things—and men—into orbit, and on the moon. As soon as they discovered Earth, the team put in a call into Peacekeeper command, registering the location of the system. From that moment on, the entire Sol system has been off limits to everyone. This will continue until the GC lifts the ban, or the occupants of the system venture far enough out to make contact.

After that, Peacekeeper patrols have only ever caught two ships trespassing near Earth. Both were pirates, hoping to loot some treasures from a protected world. Both were punished, severely. No other ships have been found in the system.

The Reaper and her captain knew better than their unlucky counterparts, staying in the outer planets' orbits, where the Peace-keepers were less likely to scan or observe ships coming and going. It helped that Lanksham only used the system to hide or wait for meetings. And that is exactly how he found Wil.

PART TWO

CHAPTER 5

A JOB IS A JOB

Two days into FTL, Wil has the computer assemble the crew in the lounge again. When he arrives, everyone is already there, waiting.

"Okay, right," Wil says. "We're all here. I have to say, this is the first time since I got the *Ghost* that it's been more than just me for more than a few days. It's kinda nice, so, you know, don't screw that up." He looks right at Bennie, who affects a stricken look on his large-eyed face.

"What? What did I do?" Bennie screeches, then dodges a pillow launched by Zephyr.

"Settle down, you animals!" Wil raises his voice. "And Bennie, whatever you are, you're part plant right?"

"Because I'm green!? You racist prick!" Bennie plops down into his chair, glaring at Wil, then Zephyr and Maxim, and back to Wil again.

"Kidding! Calm down. You're so sensitive." Wil smiles at the two Palorians, then winks at Bennie. "Look, we need talk about the job I accepted."

Zephyr and Maxim look at each other. "What job?" They say, simultaneously.

Then they look at Bennie, who just shrugs. "I was with you two on Fury, remember? How would I know?"

"It's the job I took while you two were shopping," Wil says. "Before getting chased by your former colleagues. The job we'll need to do to get the ship's accounts back to a point that doesn't make me lose sleep, and that lets us get ramped up with what we need, now that it's not just me."

"Ok, so what's the job?" Zephyr is leaning forward, hands clasped, interested.

"A snatch-and-grab from one of our employer's rivals. There's a small station in the Barsoom sector, mostly a depot for folks to store things, away from the prying eyes of the authorities."

"What authorities?" Maxim asks.

"All of them," Wil answers, dryly. "Apparently most of the major crime bosses and syndicates rent space on the station. Only they know where it is, or how to get aboard."

"What're we stealing?" Bennie seems interested. "Valuable? Tech?"

"No idea. I try to ask as few questions as I can where Xarrix is concerned. Here's what I know: the station is in the Barsoom sector, sitting out in open space. From what I'm told there's a central reception area, well guarded by a private security firm, that answers to none of the clients. Whatever it is that Xarrix wants, it's being kept on the station, in a section one of his competitors owns." A hologram begins hovering over the coffee table, and then rotates and zooms in. Wil continues: "Xarrix gave me a transponder ID that, once we're in the hold, should help ID the crate we want. But first we'll need to get to the right hold. Apparently, there'll be trace isotopes we can scan for, but only in close—and I mean like at each door close—proximity. We'll have to go door-to-door to find the right one, before breaking into it."

Wil looks at Bennie. "That's where you come in. I thought I'd have to hire a hacker when I took the gig, but thanks to a lucky turn of events, you're here." He smiles at the surly Brailack.

"I can do that."

"You don't even know what's involved," Zephyr says, looking over at Bennie.

"Doesn't matter, I'm that good." The little hacker leans back in the chair, crossing his arms behind his head.

Wil smiles. "That leaves the three of us. We're the muscle. I can get us into the central reception area, but from there, Bennie will have to hack in and lead the way. If possible, I'd rather this be more a burglary than a fight. If it turns into a fight, we're screwed."

Zephyr and Maxim look at each other, then at Wil. It is Zephyr who speaks up. "Well, I doubt you were worried, but we're in."

"I wasn't, since it wasn't optional. Okay then, step one: we case the joint." Wil zooms in further on the hologram. "This map is as accurate as any that exists, I'm told. Technically none actually exist. This was pieced together from various visits." He points to a lower portion. "This is the docking section—the station can handle four ships at once, but according to Xarrix, the protocol is only to allow one ship at a time to dock."

Maxim points to something. "Looks like only one lift connects the two sections. That's a dangerous choke point."

Wil nods. "Agreed. Hopefully, if needed, Bennie can hijack the lift controls." At this, Bennie nods.

The view moves up to the reception and vault area. It's a large circle, two levels tall. In the center is what looks like a control console, marked as 'security.' The lower level has eleven vault doors; the second tier has twelve, equally spaced around the perimeter. The two levels are connected by a staircase.

The team spends the next three tocks looking over the plans, talking through ideas. Then a beep comes from Wil's wrist comm. "We're getting close. Let's go see our prey." He stands and heads toward the bridge, and the others follow.

CASING THE JOINT

The Barsoom system isn't a very well-known one. It doesn't contain any habitable planets, and there is only one gas giant, so it's not worth fielding a mining effort. In other words, it's exactly the place you'd want to hide a secret storehouse of criminal loot, so it's precisely the place a secret storehouse of illegal loot is.

The station, for obvious reasons, isn't listed on any of the navigational charts, and its reactors are shielded so that a passing ship—should one ever venture into the Barsoom system—wouldn't even notice the station. As if that wasn't enough, it is painted black, because why not.

"Are you sure we're in the right place?" Zephyr asks, from her position on the bridge, where she is serving as unofficial first officer. Her station is configured to manage ship systems as well as the sensors and communications.

"It's there. We're still stealthed, right? I don't want them seeing us lurking around the outer edge of the system." Wil looks over at Bennie, whose station has been heavily modified in the last two days. The small Brailack is hardly visible behind all the equipment.

"Yup, we're fully stealthed and running passive right now,"

Bennie answers. "I'm looking for signals, but their game is good—not a thing out here but background radiation."

Wil adjusts the ship's heading and gooses the sub-light drive a little, to get them heading along a tangent to the station—or, at least, the supposed location of the station. The *Ghost* has two modes of propulsion. The sub-light drive, which works in space, but not in an atmosphere, can drive the ship nearly to the speed of light. Just off the center of the body of the ship on either side of the sub-light engines, the atmospheric engines are immensely powerful and can provide enough of a push to propel the ship. The design of the *Ghost* doesn't provide for atmospheric lift, so the forward section of each FTL engine boom has a repulsor field generator, which provides the lift to keep the ship in the air.

"As long as the stealth systems stay active, we can skip a cold coast, but keep an eye on it." Bennie nods in response. To Zephyr, Wil adds, "Keep an eye on the passives. This gets a lot harder if they've seen us before we arrive." She nods too.

It might not have been a cold coast, but it still takes four hours before they see anything to make them suspect they are in the right place. In theory, they should be a billion or so kilometers from the station, with it down well and themselves up well. Not that it matters this far out in the system, somewhere around the orbit of the fifth and second-to-last planet in the system. At this distance from the system's sun, it's easy to hold a position with minimal effort.

"Got something!" Zephyr announces, looking up from her station to check the main display, which she's sending data to. The screen shifts from the default view (forward, just stars as far as Wil can see) to what she is looking at on her own screens. It looks like infrared, and the whole screen is almost entirely black, but in the dead center there's a slight red-orange-black color, no bigger than Wil's fist. "We're still pretty far, so can't get much without going active, but this is from our infrared sensors. That's got to be the station. They shield the reactors so you can't pick up the radiation and energy, but it's hard to dissipate heat completely. Though I admit they seem to have gotten a pretty good system going."

Wil squints at the screen. "Wow, yeah, that's pretty impressive heat management. Ok, that's gotta be our target. Bennie, anything yet as far as signals? We're close enough to see their reactor heat—surely there's something?"

Bennie looks up from his console and shakes his head, "Nothing. Not a stray wrist comm ping, or unsecured transceiver. That place is a black box."

"Ok, that's not good. Might have to adjust our plan."

Maxim has been silent for hours, so silent that Wil jumps when the big ex-Peacekeeper now speaks. "Why does the plan change?" Maxim is sitting at the weapons station, which in the ship's current state is purely for show—all weapons are completely powered down, including targeting scanners.

"Might have to get you a bell to wear!" Wil says. "If they're keeping that tight a lid on signals, I'm guessing they've got the whole place set up as a Faraday cage. The instant we're aboard, we won't be able to communicate with Bennie here on the ship and vice-versa. The whole plan revolves around him getting into their system and guiding us." Wil leans forward in his chair, staring at the main view screen and the bruise-colored smudge in the center.

"I might have a solution." Maxim offers.

[2] This refers to the gravity well, with "down" being closer to the star, "up" being further away.

THE PLAN

Wil looks at the big Palorian. "Go for it, big man. What ya thinking?"

Maxim looks over at Zephyr. "Remember the mission to the Dralobian embassy? We had to have our hacker guide us through."

Zephyr nods, understanding crossing her features. "Yes, I think that could work! Let me look over the plans Xarrix provided Wil."

Wil looks at one, then the other. "Mind sharing?"

Zephyr gestures to Maxim to continue. The ex-Peacekeeper shifts in his chair. "Our squad was sent to infiltrate the Dralobian embassy on Rostham Four. We didn't know the layout of the structure, since they imported an all-Dralobian workforce to build it, and the only known plans were in the secure server, on the inside. The Peacekeepers wanted to bug the facility and get a complete blueprint, so we needed to infiltrate the building, access the server, and copy the files. Our squad hacker faced the same problem we do: the embassy was immensely secure, so the onsite security forces would detect our comms instantly. That meant she had to be onsite, too."

"So?" Wil asks.

"So we engineered a minor disaster in the building—something to do with the plumbing. That way the embassy had to allow our hover van onto the property. From there we were able to park close enough to a data access junction and splice a hardwired connection."

Wil roll-waves his hand, in what he assumes is a universal gesture for *keep going*.

"So, since we're going to have to dock with the station anyway, unless there's a shuttle bay on this thing, I haven't found..." Wil shakes his head. "Perfect. And when we're docked, it shouldn't be that hard to find a data access junction somewhere near the docking section. Bennie can access the station that way. On top of that, then he can likely hide our comms inside the system, so there are no extraneous signals to raise suspicion." Wil looks over at Bennie. "Will that work?"

The little hacker grins evilly—an immensely disturbing sight. "Yeah, that'd be just fine. I can do a lot more with a hardline connection. As long as there's a junction."

"Yes, here we go." Zephyr updates the primary display with the plans Xarrix has provided. "If this is accurate, the central docking section has four docking arms. Since we assume we'll be the only ship there, the entire section will be empty, save us. We're lucky Xarrix was thorough—these plans are quite detailed." The image zooms in. "Here you can see a primary data access junction. I'm sure it's locked, but that shouldn't be an issue. From there we can set Bennie up just inside the docking arm."

"What about cameras? Surely the central docking section isn't that insecure." Wil uses his station to zoom the image back out and pan it around, looking for the symbols that would indicate a camera or sensor cluster.

"You're not thinking like a criminal, Wil," Zephyr says. "This station is super secure, super anonymous. There are guards in the reception area, which other than the docking section is the only public space. The guard's silence can be—and likely is—bought. Digital evidence of customer comings and goings would be bad for business. If just one customer hacks the station, they'll know who all the other clients are, when they come and go, and what type of crates they're moving. I wonder how Xarrix accomplished this."

"Good point, and you probably don't want to know. Okay, I think we've got a workable plan here, lady and gentlemen... Bennie, you're a male right?"

The already surly Brailack turns a deeper shade of green. "The hell do you mean, 'am I a male?' What the hell did you think I was?!?"

Wil raises both hands, palms out. "Okay, okay, you know, just trying to be sensitive and not make assumptions." He ducks just in time to keep from getting a PADD to the face.

THE BREAK IN

The voice comes clearly over the bridge loudspeakers: "Unidentified craft, you have thirty fractions of a tock to transmit your identity and access documents."

"Friendly," mutters Maxim.

"Bennie, you have the doctored ID ready to go?" Wil asks, from the pilot seat in the center of the bridge.

Bennie looks over at Wil and gives a thumbs up. At least, Wil assumes that's what it's supposed to be—it's harder to tell on a three-fingered hand. Wil reaches for the communications controls on his own station. "Station, this is transport *Serenity*, transmitting ID and access documents now." Wil looks at his new and untested—at least as a unit—crew. "Here we go."

It takes the station about five minutes to go over the transmitted documents. All the while the *Ghost* is getting closer and closer. "They're still targeting us," Maxim warns from the weapons station. "Should we target them back?"

Wil shakes his head. "No, we're transmitting doctored-up ID docs, as well as a doctored sensor image. Unless someone looks out the window, we're just a mid-sized transport. If we start painting them with all kinds of targeting scans, they might look closer. Besides,

I have to assume any transport trusted enough to come out here would know how it works, and wouldn't worry about it. I hope."

"Reassuring," Maxim grumbles.

The speakers crackle slightly. "*Serenity*. Everything checks out; you're clear to dock at Docking Collar Three."

"They're no longer targeting us," Maxim reports, with visible relief.

Wil begins guiding the ship to its assigned docking collar. "Okay, you two: go get ready." He nods at Maxim and Zephyr. "Bennie, you too."

As the ex-Peacekeepers exit the bridge, Bennie turns to Wil. "You know, this would be easier if we'd done my shopping first. Just saying."

Wil doesn't take his eyes off his displays. "I haven't decided if you get to stay on my ship, and I'm not wasting a single credit on your green ass until then."

Bennie scowls at the back of Wil's head, and leaves the bridge.

Ten minutes later, Wil walks the short distance from the bridge to the portside airlock, located on the forward section of the ship, just behind the bridge. The main receiving area between both airlocks has been modified to be a more military-grade staging area. A few racks of weapons and body armor line the front and back walls, with short walkways to each side, leading to the airlocks.

Walking in, Wil finds two Peacekeepers in full Peacekeeper combat armor. "What the... we're sneaking aboard the station, not storming Normandy!"

The larger armor-clad form asks, "What's Normandy?" Then the visor snaps up revealing a slightly grinning Maxim.

Wil shakes his head. "Where did you even *get* all that? I know the budget I gave you wouldn't include weapons AND two full sets of Peacekeeper armor."

The smaller armored form turns to Wil, and the faceplate snaps up, revealing Zephyr. "We got creative with the budget. Also, the weapons dealer hadn't found a buyer in three cycles, so was a bit desperate to get rid of these. They're not current gen, but they're good enough. Also, if you want to sneak, this is what you want." She taps a few controls on her gauntlet, and fades from view, as the face-plate drops back over her face, sealing her into her armor. "Prismatic, adaptive camouflage." At best, Wil can just make out a faint wavering outline.

"Okay, one: kudos on the creative budgeting. Two: Zephyr, stay in yours. Max, sorry, but I need you to be visible muscle. Remember our cover is we're here making a drop for Xarrix. We're gonna have to have a cargo crate to lug around, and we need to look like lowlife cargo runners."

"Maxim. My name is Maxim," the big Palorian grumbles as he begins disassembling his armor. Zephyr returns to visibility and moves to help him.

Wil puts his hand on the big man's shoulder. "Next time, I promise you get to wear armor, deal?"

Maxim nods. Wil turns to the section of the room where he keeps his own gear, and grabs his utility belt and an extra sidearm. He also takes a gauntlet designed to go over his wrist comm—not only protecting it but adding to its abilities. "Where's Bennie?" Wil tilts his head up to the ceiling. "Computer, where's Bennie?"

"I'm right here!" Bennie says, coming from the direction of the main corridor. "I had to gear up." He's loaded down with—well, Wil has no idea what, but every pocket and pouch on the jumpsuit the little guy likes to wear is packed with stuff. Also, he's buried under a large backpack.

"What is all that? You're going to be 5 meters from the ship, at most. Not stranded on a deserted island." Wil shakes his head, but decides it's not worth arguing about. "Okay, everyone ready? Remember the plan?"

Nodding all around.

"Okay, then. Let's go rob somebody."

Wil has no idea what's going on; his head is swimming, he's got about a million questions, and he doesn't know what's happening around him, with so many aliens moving. He's following along behind Lanksham, and his two—what? Guards? They still haven't spoken, but they haven't left the Captain's side, either. Wil is between them, as they walk together down a corridor of some type.

Ahead, a hatch opens, sliding apart. They walk into what Wil guesses is the bridge. There's a central seat and stations all around it —some of them are occupied, some aren't. The two guards take positions at two of the stations. *Guess they're more than just muscle,* Wil thinks. Lanksham sits in the center, in what looks like a cross between Captain Kirk's chair and the cockpit of Wil's pod, sans the pod itself. The captain must also fly the ship.

Pressing a button on his console, Lanksham says, "Gartrath, is the hold secured?" A *yes* comes back over the bridge speakers, and Lanksham pushes some buttons and takes the controls. Wil can see the stars moving in the display at the front of the room. A second later, the stars vanish and a swirling effect replaces them. Lanksham gets up from his station and heads for the hatch they recently entered through. "Come with me," he says, pushing past Wil and making a gesture to his two crewmen—crew beings?—that he doesn't need them this time.

They walk back down the same corridor, which must be the only way to the bridge, Wil guesses. A turn and then they're in a largish space, not the cargo hold. Wil has no idea how big the ship is, or its layout. He had thought they were going back to the cargo hold and his pod, but somehow they have ended up in this lounge area.

Sitting in a large overstuffed chair, Lanksham points to a smaller chair opposite his. "Most would have either left you in your pod to die, or brought you aboard, then spaced you and kept your pod."

"Uh, thanks?"

"You're human, ya? This system is where your home planet is."

"Yeah, Earth. Third planet from the sun, our star."

"Yeah, so I'm breaking a ton of rules, but figure that's better than letting you die. Fact is, this system—especially the inner orbits—are off limits. No ifs, ands, or buts. Get caught here, and the Peace-keepers take your ship, toss you in one of their holes, and that's that." Lanksham strokes his beard—it looks like hair, but who knows. "Since we were here and I'm not a complete block of ice, we grabbed you on our way out. That's the good news; you get to live. The bad news is you'll probably never go home."

Wil opens his mouth to protest, ask questions, possibly scream incoherently. Lanksham raises a six-fingered hand to stop him. "It sucks, I know. I can't take you home, and no one else ever will either —the punishment is too severe, especially going that far in system. Maybe one day you'll have a ship, but what then? You go home on your own? I don't know much about your people, but if they're anything like 98% of the other races in this sector, your government will have no end of questions. They'll likely dissect you, and then just as likely either use the ship you come in, or reverse engineer it. In either of those cases, the moment your people start venturing out of your system the GC ban is lifted. That means your people are as likely to find pirates and slavers as peaceful well-meaning folks. Best not accelerate the process until your people are ready." Lanksham stands up and walks over to some refrigerator-looking thing and grabs two bottles. Sitting back down, he leans forward and hands one to Wil.

"Life sucks, and yours is about to get worse before it gets better." He takes a long pull on his drink. Wil sniffs the top of the bottle and follows suit. *Tastes kinda like beer*, he decides. "Until I get tired of you, or find someone to pawn you off on, you're part of my crew. The *Reaper* isn't a big ship, but we get by. Oh, and in case you haven't put it together, this," waving to encompass the entire space, "is the *Reaper*. She's an Ankarran Raptor, which I know means nothing to you—but believe me, that's impressive. We do what we can to stay flying. Smuggling, a little piracy, but never slaving, that dren is despicable. We haul cargo sometimes when it pays enough. Sometimes we do mercenary work. Like I said, whatever keeps us flying. Everyone pulls their weight; everyone shares the risks, everyone gets a cut of the action." Taking another drink of the beer like drink, he asks, "Any questions?"

Wil sits there for a beat, holding his beer-like drink, staring at Lanksham, and then he screams. When he stops Lanksham smiles. "Feel better?"

"Not really, but if I didn't let that out, I might have exploded. I don't even know what to say or what to ask. It sounds like I don't have much say in the matter, so, you know, I don't know what else to say."

Lanksham nods. "You're handling this better than I expected, I won't lie. Maybe because you're one of your planets explorers, this is all easier to grasp. I don't know, but I'm glad you're not a blubbering mess. This type of thing isn't exactly routine, but it's happened enough, there are stories. Sad—mine will be boring, come to think of it."

Wil rubs at his face, thinking. "Okay. My first question is, how are you speaking English, or am I speaking your language? Do you have a universal translator?"

"That's a weird name, but quite accurate. You're speaking whatever you speak; I'm speaking my language. The computer is translating. That's why it's a little laggy. The rest of us have translator microbes." Lanksham gestures vaguely toward his head. "You'll get some soon, and it'll be easier."

"That's good; this has been a surreal and terrifying kung-fu movie, so far." Wil sets his bottle down. "Am I a slave?"

"Weren't you listening? I don't do that. It's despicable. No, you're not a slave. You're crew. Low-ranking for sure, like a cabin boy. You have to earn your place, but you're crew."

Wil thinks about it for a second. "Well, that's good. I guess."

Over the speakers, a voice: "Captain, we're almost to Gupta. ETA point five tocks."

Lanksham looks to the ceiling. "I'll be there shortly." Turning his attention to Wil, he says, "We'll continue this later, but for now we have business to attend to. Come with me. You can stay on the bridge and watch, but don't touch anything."

CHAPTER 6

THE BREAK-IN: BENNIE

"Okay Bennie, you're gonna be on your own. You got this?" Wil is kneeling in front of the little hacker, just inside the airlock of the *Ghost*.

"Yeah, I got this," Bennie snaps. "You guys do your thing. Remember to keep the channel open so that I can reach you. Also, you know I'm probably older than you— what's with the kneeling down like I'm a kid?"

The three walk out of the airlock. Wil glances back over his shoulder. "We'll be waiting for your signal." Then the lift door closes.

Bennie looks around the docking area. "Time to get to work," he mutters to himself, and runs over to where the blueprints indicate the primary data access junction is located.

Except there's nothing there. "Oh, grolack." He looks around, frantically. The docking area isn't especially large—just a circular room, with a lift and four identical docking collar hatches. Three have a red light over them, while the one attached to the *Ghost* has a green light.

"OK, Ben-Ari, calm down. Think this through. We know there was a primary data access junction in this area. Even if they got rid of the access panel, those data conduits are still here—they have to be. So, where are they?"

He looks around, but the wall where the panel should be is perfectly smooth. Whatever modifications they'd made included a complete replacement of the bulkhead, not just welding the panel shut. His eyes slowly roam around the room.

"The *floor!!*" Bennie goes back to where the panel should have been and examines the floor. It's a mix of solid metal plates, and grates. Grates! Sure enough, about a meter from the bulkhead is a metal grate—and beneath it, data conduits! He drops to his knees and grabs at the grate, attempting to lift it. It's heavy; well, it's not so much heavy as Bennie isn't strong. Grunting and straining, he moves the grate inch by inch, until it's moved enough for him to reach into the opening.

He grabs his gear and starts getting set up. He's glad that when he fled his workshop on Fury, he'd taken his portable deck since the equipment on the *Ghost* is woefully inadequate for this task, and not at all portable. Reaching into the opening in the floor, he clips a few jack clamps to various conduits—better safe than sorry, so he'll tap everything. The sound of the jack clamps burning through the conduit soon comes from the floor, followed by the faint smell of burnt plastic. Jack clamps are a hackers dream; each one, once connected automatically, begins burning through the conduit insulation, and attaches a lead to the exposed data cable. The edges of the clamp then super-heat and form an airtight seal so that the tap is completely secure.

"Ok, here we go." Bennie connects the opposite ends of the jack clamp cables into the back of his portable deck, and lights come on around each port, indicating a stable connection. "Excellent."

Sitting cross-legged on the floor, the little hacker gets to work. The security systems in place around the station are numerous. Whoever designed this station did a great job of making sure the data core was well protected. The first hurdle will be getting past the firewalls around the main docking area. This was clearly something someone was worried about when they designed the system. Bennie chuckles as he watches his firewall countermeasure routines dismantle and reassemble the firewall around the chamber—leaving a nice wide opening for him to get one level up, into the main reception area, while outwardly still looking completely intact.

This second tier, however, is much more involved. Not only is there a firewall protecting data access on that level, there's one on each vault door, and another protecting the central guard station. From what Bennie can see, the vault doors will be easier to deal with if he can take over the guard station. "This might be harder than I expected. Hold on, guys," he says to himself, since he hasn't cracked the internal comm system yet.

He frowns, concentrating on the guard station. Clearly whoever built and designed this station was familiar with the most likely vectors of system attack. "You're good, that's clear, but I'm better," the Brailack chuckles, as the first level of the guard station computer defenses crumbles under the onslaught of various viruses that Bennie is unleashing. The trick is not to simply brute force the attack, because then the system will realize that it's under attack and raise the alarm. While the viruses are cracking the defense systems, Bennie is busy attacking lower-level systems like communications, to keep the guard kiosk systems from raising the alarm. So far so good.

"Yes!!!" The little hacker throws both arms in the air. "You can't beat Ben-Ari! Oh, dren!" His hands fly back to the console. "Okay, okay, I see what you did, that's clever." A few tabs on the deck, and the guard station, now belong to Bennie. His smile is huge and slightly evil looking.

"Okay, got the guard kiosk, so... where would you... Ah! There you are. Internal comms. Okay, just need to find a channel that's unused... there we go." Some tapping and working menus on the deck. "Okay, now, to be extra safe, ensure there's no buffer storage, then... Right, here we go, channel encrypted." He taps some more, then taps the comms button on his deck. "Is this thing on?"

THE BREAK-IN: WIL

The lift doors open into the main reception area, Wil and Maxim step out, the former pushing a heavy looking crate on a grav-sled. Two well armed and armored security guards are waiting for them

"This way." The taller of the two says, pointing towards the center of the reception area, where two more guards are sitting at a central kiosk. If the reception area were a clock, the lift from the docking area would be the six o'clock position, and every hour would be a secure vault door, stacked two high, twenty-three vaults for Zephyr to check.

Wil and Maxim walk toward the center of the room, the first pair of guards falling in line behind them, not noticing a slight shimmer that slips out of the lift once everyone's back is turned.

"Hey there, guys!" Wil exclaims when they get to the central guard station. "How's it going? Quite some station you have here. Do you live here or is there some kind of shuttle service or something?"

The guards look at each other, then back at Wil. One puts his hand out, "Documents."

Wil hands over a data chip with the forged and hopefully believable documents Xarrix had provided. Luckily, as with all good lies, there was some truth. Xarrix has a vault on this station and has the right to send anyone he likes to make deposits and withdrawals.

The first guard looks up from the terminal in front of him, "Your documents check out. You know what to do?"

Wil looks around, "Uh, actually no, this is my first time doing this run." He looks at Maxim behind the crate, "You know what to do?"

Maxim shakes his head.

"Mute, can you imagine how boring the trip out here was. I mean, I don't mind talking to myself, but this place ain't close to anything. It was a long flight, and of course, since it's a secret and all, no other crew. Boring is too gentle a word." Wil says, shaking his head, "You mind showing us the process?"

The guard grumbles and gets up from his seat, "Come on." Wil goes to follow, and Maxim, with the crate, turns as well. Two steps and the grav-sled makes a weird and not at all good sounding noise, and drops six inches to the ground with a loud thud. "What the hell?! I thought you fixed it?" Wil looks at Maxim, who shrugs and shakes his head. Wil punches him in the arm, then jumps back at the glare he receives. The guard has spun on his heals and is eyeing the two suspiciously. The other guard, at the kiosk, is also standing.

"I don't believe this." the nearest guard says to the other. "How does this dren always happen to us? Jareth and Boxter grolacking read, and we get these two idiots." He turns to Wil, "No offense."

"None taken." Wil smiles and kneels to work on the grave sled. "That said, this would go faster if you helped, or at least have tools? I could go get them from the ship, but I'd have to find 'em."

The least angry guard grabs a small pack from the guard kiosk and walks around to help Wil and Maxim.

From Wil's earpiece, "This thing on?" Wil barely manages to not jump out of his skin. He'd forgotten Bennie was going to do that. Just then there's a clang. Everyone stops moving. The guards all react like professionals, weapons up, visually scanning the room. The two from the elevator head for the stairwell that leads to the second level.

THE BREAK-IN: ZEPHYR

As soon as Wil and Maxim have stepped out of the lift, Zephyr has darted out after them, sliding to the side of the room. Now she's standing in front of the first of the vaults, realizing the size of the task ahead of her. Luckily, she knows she can't be seen. Peacekeeper combat armor—even older models like the one Zephyr is wearing—are state of the art, compared to what almost anyone else can get their hands on. Being designed and built in-house, the specs never leave Peacekeeper control. In the field, damaged units internally self-destruct, destroying all internal components, rendering the suit a weighty piece of trash— how this suit and the one Maxim has survived that, Zephyr doesn't know. The internal systems are completely self-contained, and the suit and its occupant can survive just about any environment for several hours. Peacekeeper armor—regardless of class or mission parameter—is designed to hide the wearer's identity. Once a Peacekeeper is in their armor, you can't tell gender or even height, as most armor is the same size, internally cushioning shorter operators. The Prismatic adaptive camouflage allows a Peacekeeper to walk right past security systems effectively.

The lift arrives at the reception deck and the doors open. There are two guards right by the lift, on each side of the door, "This way," one of them says to Wil and Maxim. They follow the guards toward the center of the room. Just as the lift doors close, Zephyr slips out.

Since the identity of the vault owners isn't known to anyone on the station, there's no record of who owns which vault. Zephyr needs to identify the target vault with a small scanner that should—from what Xarrix told Wil—identify some trace isotopes he slipped onto his competitor the last time they were in the same place. Apparently, shortly before, said competitor had headed for this station. That's a lot more 'ifs' and 'shoulds' than Zephyr is comfortable with.

She slips out the lift to one side and heads for the first door. This is going to take some time, she realizes. Fortunately, she was able to confirm the isotopes presence in the lift, so that was good—so far, Xarrix's intel is correct. Unfortunately, however, the isotope is too weak to leave a trail from the lift to the vault she's looking for. Likely she'll only be able to find a small trace of it, on the vault control pad.

"Hey there, guys!" Wil exclaims from across the room. Now the hard part: he and Maxim have to do as much as they can to slow things down, while Zephyr looks for the right vault, and Bennie takes control of the station's systems.

She moves to another vault door—nothing on the scanner, dren. The scanner can't pick up the isotope unless it's within a limited range, which means she has to stand in front of each door while the scanner works.

She's almost done with the first floor when she hears a loud thud, and sees the grav-sled and crate crash to the ground. She watches Wil and Maxim flail about, and lure all four guards in closer. So far so good.

Time to head upstairs. She's about halfway up the steps, when without warning she hears: "This thing on?" Despite years of Peacekeeper training, she's startled, and her foot catches the stair, making a clanging sound as she catches her grip. She freezes.

THE BREAK-IN: WIL

Wil and Maxim exchange glances when the guard helping them turns away. "Uh, ya'll got space rats or something?" Wil asks.

"What the grolack is a space rat?" the helpful guard asks.

"You know: small, furry, tail, beady eyes, lives in space. Space rat." Wil is holding his hands about six inches apart. "Sneak aboard ships, eat wires, shit everywhere."

"Be quiet!" the angry guard snaps. He and the helpful one have spread out around the lower level. Wil and Maxim trade glances again.

The guards are moving fast—the first two are already at the stairwell now, heading up. The other two are doing a circuit around the outer level of the reception area and first level of vault doors. They stop near each door, probably interfacing with the door mechanism, so see if any of the doors are reporting an error or alert.

Using the subvocalization capabilities of the comms gear, he whispers: "It's on, Bennie. But I think you startled Zephyr—gods knows you scared me. Guards are doing a circuit around the place. Hold tight."

"Oops, sorry about that! I guess I shoulda had the comms do a tone to let you know it was coming online. Next time," Bennie replies. "So, I'm through most of the firewalls. I've got control of the guard kiosk and all its systems. I'm trying to figure out how to open the vault doors, for when Zephyr finds the right one. How long can you stall?"

"Uh, what? Not long, they're already getting pretty pissy. As soon as they're done making sure there's nothing going, which I hope happens soon, they'll be pushing to get this grav-sled fixed and get us moving."

Just then Zephyr chimes in. "Sorry for the noise. Bennie's isn't a voice that should suddenly pop into your thoughts. I'm on the second level—I was able to get the rest of the way up the steps before the guards came up here. It looks like they're almost done. I'm starting my sweep now."

On the second level walkway, Wil can see the two guards nearing the stairwell from opposite sides.

"Okay, go as quick as you can—I don't think we're gonna have long. The vault we need being upstairs is gonna be a problem. How quietly can you move, when you're moving fast?"

A faint beep comes over the line. "Not that one, still looking. I guess we'll find out soon on the fast and quiet thing."

The guards that stayed on the same level are back. "Hey, you get that thing working, yet?"

Wil bangs around for a few minutes, grunting occasionally. He holds a hand up, one finger extended in the universal *one more minute gesture*. After another few bangs, he closes the hatch on the grav-sled, and looks up, no idea if it's angry guard or helpful who's waiting for an answer. "Yeah I think so, what was it? Space rats?"

No answer—and with the face masks being jet black, no indication the guard even registered the question beyond a slight tilting of his head.

Wil hands Maxim the tools, and presses a button on the control panel. The sled beeps a few times, then slowly lifts. Since the grav-sled was never actually broken, just cleverly modified to fail on command, fixing it was easy. "Voilà!" Wil says. *Too easy, suckers.*

"What?" That must be the helpful guard.

Maxim re-assembles the toolkit and hands it back to helpful guard. Angry guard points to Wil. "Make your deposit and get out."

"So rude." Wil makes a show of pulling out a PADD and thumbing through it, looking for the door he's supposed to go to. He looks up, then left and right, then heads toward the door that belongs to Xarrix, Maxim following, pushing the sled ahead of him.

"Bennie, Zephyr," he hisses into the comms unit. "Time's just about up. Status?"

Nothing.

"Anyone?"

Then, over his comms, comes Zephyr. "Yes! Found it."

THE BREAK-IN: ZEPHYR

Zephyr hears Wil trying to defuse the situation—something about space rats, whatever they are.

As the guards approach the staircase, she knows there's no way they'll pass her on the stairs without noticing. One of them will bump or brush against her, or pick up the telltale shimmer from the cloaking system—it's good, but not that good, up close, especially at only a matter of inches away. She has to move. Where though?

The guards are at the bottom of the stairs now. Zephyr is only five steps above them. Carefully, she times her steps with theirs, to mask the sound. She assumes that they'll split up when they hit the top of the stairs, which leaves only one place to go...

As soon as she reaches the top of the stairs, she leaps over the edge of the walkway. Relying on her years of training, she grabs the railing with one hand to control her trajectory and slow her fall. She pivots and catches herself with her other hand; thankfully the armor enhances her strength, as she hovers ninety degrees out from the railing. Quickly, she instructs the armor to go rigid, letting her relax her arms. The two guards hit the top of the stairs, confer briefly then split up and start slowly moving from vault door to vault door.

Zephyr waits until both guards are three doors away before she hauls herself back up and over the railing as quietly as possible. She heads for the nearest vault door, speaking quietly into the comms unit. "Sorry for the noise..."

She turns to the door nearest the top of the stairs: nothing. Then she moves to the next. The guards are both almost opposite her. They're not on the alert for anything, other than generally looking for things out of place, which mostly means just glancing at the control panel for each vault door, confirming its display information, and then moving on.

Over the comms Wil says, "Okay, go as quick as you can—I don't think we're gonna have long. The vault we need being upstairs is gonna be a problem. How quietly can you move, when you're moving fast?"

Another door, negative on the scanner. Zephyr hisses in frustration.

Glancing down at the reception area, it looks like time's up: Wil and Maxim are moving toward what she assumes is their door. "Dren," she mutters. She can only move so fast without making any noise. Her armor can warp light but doesn't muffle much sound. At least the guards that had been up on this level are back on the stairs now, heading down together.

She moves to another door: nothing. The next door: nothing.

Wil, on comms: "Bennie, Zephyr, time's just about up. Status?"

Next door: nothing. She keeps moving—fearing the door she's looking at will be the last one she hits; knowing there's nothing she can do about.

"Anyone?" Wil's voice asks.

She moves to the next door, and the sensor makes a different noise. "Yes! Found it."

THE BREAK-IN: BENNIE

Bennie hears Wil asking the guards, "Uh, y'all got space rats or something?" and snickers to himself.

Humans say such goofy things, Bennie thinks. He wishes this place had cameras on the upper levels; he doesn't like not being able to see what's going on.

"How long can you stall?" he asks, looking through the various directories in the guard kiosk. Whoever designed this place didn't trust their clientele, and didn't trust their hired goons, either. The systems are heavily shielded, both externally as well as internally. Bennie's respect for the architect of this station's security and computer systems is growing by the moment, as is his determination to beat those same systems.

While Wil and Zephyr talk Bennie, tunes them out and focuses. He's got to be ready when she finds the right vault, but these systems are so spread out and locked down, it's not as easy as he'd assumed.

Muting his wrist comm, he mutters to himself, "This is promising —there's no direct per-vault override, but... Hmm, yeah, this is promising."

Bennie digs into the systems he's exploring, setting aside

programs for later use, burying routines throughout the data core, and assigning hot keys and macros.

Crucial minutes pass, and he's still buried in the various systems —admiring the craftsmanship, taking note of clever bits of code, and well-crafted subroutines, dismantling things as politely as he can.

Then he notices the comm light flashing. "Oops!" Quickly, he clicks it on.

"Anyone?" It's Wil, sounding panicked.

"Sorry, I'm here. I think I have something that will work." Bennie taps a few more commands into his deck, nods to himself. "Yes, this will work. Say the word."

Just then Zephyr comes over the comms. "Yes! Found it."

CHAPTER 7

THE BREAK-IN: BENNIE

Wil's voice comes over the comms: "Okay—then, *go!*"

Bennie hits a button on his deck, mapped to a series of commands he has programmed in. He knows exactly what will happen now.

First, his routines will take over the environmental controls, making the system think there is an environmental emergency. Then a series of viruses take over the guard systems, killing all the sensors, while plunging them into an unending feedback loop.

Even though there aren't sensors in the vaults to monitor what goes on, there are standard safety sensors—which can, luckily, be tricked into thinking there's someone trapped in each vault and that the oxygen is leaving those vaults. This triggers the doors to every vault, snapping them open.

Despite the anti-intrusion and privacy setup, the creators of this station either forgot to eliminate these safety protocols or hedged their bets, deciding that clients dying in one of their vaults wouldn't be good press. Killing the main power is even easier—those systems are protected, but not well—so killing the lights is easy. Putting the life support into a forced reboot interrupts that for at least a few minutes—more if he can keep on interrupting the system.

That's only part of the problem though, the easiest part. The four guards are all in self-powered armor, which will have night vision and advanced sensors. The lights being out won't do much to them; they'll still see Wil and Maxim if they try anything. Not good.

The solution took as much doing—more, maybe—as the hacking of the environmental controls. Bennie had found, buried deep in the guard kiosk protocols, a data link to all active guards. This link was intended to allow the guards to all share data with the kiosk, including sensor feeds and so forth, allowing the station's computer to monitor input from each guard as they patrol, compiling the data into an accurate picture of the station overall.

It is all the crack in the armor Bennie needs.

He rapidly executes another set of routines that make quick work of the weak firewall protecting the data pathway to the guard uniforms. And then... he's in.

He immediately accesses all four guards' armor, specifically their helmet systems. He'd simply lock their whole suit down, paralyzing them, if that wasn't too obvious. So instead, he's going to crash their helmets. They won't die—their life support systems will still be active—but the rest of their armor will be effectively dead, temporarily.

Without warning, up in the reception area, the guards' helmet systems go dark: no comms, no visual feeds, and—to make sure they don't take them off—the guard kiosk tells the armor that a deadly airborne pathogen has been detected, so the suits seal up completely, switching to internal life support. The guards are now blind, deaf, and locked inside their armor. Bennie can imagine all four guards immediately reaching for their helmets, trying to disengage the locking mechanisms in the collars.

"Go!" Bennie yells into the comms unit.

With part one done, he focuses on the harder part: erasing all evidence of this ever happening. Harder by far than Phase One, Phase Two is something he rarely has to worry about—he's always been able to hide his identity when hacking a system, but never bothered to erase the evidence of his trespass. Who cares if the victims know they've been hacked? Maybe next time they'll be more prepared. This time, however, it has to be as if none of this has happened—with only the guard's word to go on if the computers don't back it up. The guards won't want to lose their jobs, and likely either won't ever report this, or if they do, they'll withdraw their report when they find out there's no actual evidence of the incident.

"Bennie, you almost ready?" Wil asks, amid a lot grunting from someone on comms; Bennie hasn't been paying attention.

"Almost, give me a tick." He's typing furiously. It's a good thing this whole covering-your-tracks thing isn't something he usually worries about, or he'd have found a different vocation a long time ago.

"Okay, I'm ready when you are. Everything will come back online together, so be ready," he warns.

"Do it," Wil orders. Bennie hits a command on his deck, and every system he's captured is released. Quickly, subroutines he's embedded begin to erase logs, overwrite data, and do whatever else is needed to remove any evidence of his presence in the system, before deleting themselves too. He has to hurry, since Wil and the crew will be returning shortly—possibly with company. Finding him sitting there in the docking area would blow the whole operation.

He's busy erasing files and pulling back his routines when he sees the guards start to access systems. They're looking for an explanation. "Suckers," he snickers, while finishing up. As a precaution, he made sure to clean up the armor and the guard kiosk first, knowing that'd be where the guards would look first. The guards will no doubt ask the computers in their armor for a status report, and be confused when the armor reports nothing anomalous. But what's happened up there? Did they get manage to get the goods?

"Okay, that's it," he says over the comms, beginning to power down his deck. He starts unplugging his data taps. Unfortunately, if anyone looks too hard, they'll see the ends of the jack clamps that fused to the conduits. They'd have to be in 'tear the station apart' mode, though, and without a single shred of evidence to back up the guard's story, there's no reason to think that'll happen. Bennie slides the grate closed and hears the faint tone the lift makes. The doors are about to open!

He grabs his deck, and scurries as fast as he can to the airlock, turning the corner of the boarding corridor just as the lift doors open.

THE BREAK-IN: ZEPHYR

Suddenly, Wil's voice is on the comms: "Okay—then, *go!*"

The entire reception area is plunged into darkness. Zephyr's armor switches to a combination of enhanced night vision with LIDAR overlay, as the low rumble of the station's life support fades. To ensure she isn't detected, her armor has been on internal life support mode from the start—no sense letting the station's computer detect extra CO_2.

The door right in front of her snaps open. Zephyr doesn't wait—she races in, as Bennie's voice yells over the comms: "Go!"

The vault is larger than she expected, packed with crates of various sizes, and a few statues and other knick-knacks. This crime boss or crooked politician is doing well for themselves. If this is all the stuff they don't want anyone knowing about, then they must have much, much more than is publicly viewable. She sighs and gets to work: moving from crate to crate, scanning for the isotope. She's thankful that stealth isn't an issue right now. She's able to move quickly, and somewhat loudly, from crate to crate.

"I'm in and scanning," she reports. "There's more than I expected —going as fast as I can."

"You can move as fast as you like. The guards are blind and deaf right now," Bennie says.

She shakes her head, choosing to not reply to such an obvious comment.

"Which vault?" Wil asks over the comms. "We'll get in position."

"Fifth from the top of the stairs to the right," she answers.

Thankfully, whoever owns this vault is organized: no crates blocking other crates, very few stacked more than two high, nothing likely to topple if touched. Zephyr moves in a methodical search pattern, passing her scanner over each crate, looking for a trace of that isotope.

If time weren't an issue, she'd love to look around a bit more. This vault is a true treasure trove! There's a solid platinum statue of some noble figure from the past, at least three meters tall. In the corner is what looks like a sarcophagus holding who knows what, or whom. In another corner, on a set of shelving that reaches to the ceiling, are stacks and stacks of ingots, all arranged by type of metal and lashed together in sets.

Beep. "Found it!" she reports to the team. It's a crate about half as big as the one Wil and Maxim brought in, which is good. She moves to open it. "Dren, the crate's locked."

"Gonna have to take the whole thing! Can you carry it?" Wil asks.

She grabs both sides and lifts. It's heavy, but her armor can handle the strain, at least for a little bit. "Yes, coming to you," she huffs.

She's careful not to drag the crate. Moving it isn't easy, and she wouldn't be able to without the strength augmentation her armor provides. Leaving drag marks would be a clear piece of evidence for the owner, whenever they eventually realize they've been robbed. Right below her are Wil and Maxim, and their crate. She slowly makes her way to the vault door and the railing beyond.

"Drop it," Wil calls over the comms. "Max will catch it." The two talk, then Maxim comes back on. "Okay, Zephyr, I'm ready." She lets the crate slide over the edge.

THE BREAK IN, WIL

As Wil and Maxim get to the door, the helpful guard is about twenty steps behind them, watching.

"Okay—then, *go!*" No sooner has Wil subvocalized the words do the lights go out, every single one of them. The rumble of the life support system dies off.

And every single vault door snaps open.

Then Bennie's voice on comms: "Go!"

Wil and Maxim both grab night-vision goggles from pockets in their outfits. Maxim sets about opening the crate they've been moving around this whole time; it's empty inside.

Over the comms, Zephyr reports, "I'm in and scanning. There's more than I expected—going as fast as I can."

"You can move as fast as you like. The guards are blind and deaf right now," Bennie says.

Wil looks up. "Which vault? We'll get in position."

"Fifth from the top of the stairs to the right."

Wil and Maxim get moving. Wil can see the guards spinning around: one of them has their rifle up and is waving it around. *Hope he doesn't get trigger happy*, Wil thinks. Two others are still grabbing at their helmets. The helpful guard is standing exactly where he was before, slowly turning his head. Wil looks right at him; his entire body is rigid. Wil figures he doesn't know what to do, so is staying where he was in case others are moving around. Sound idea—the other three are not that disciplined, and the two from upstairs have collided and are now floundering about on the deck.

Dodging one flailing guard, they get the crate set up under the door Zephyr has reported from. "We're in position."

A few minutes later, they hear her: "Found it! Dren, the crate is locked."

Wil looks at Maxim. "Gonna have to take the whole thing! Can you carry it?"

"Yes, coming to you," she says.

"Drop it," Wil calls back over comms. "Max will catch it."

"I will?" the large ex-Peacekeeper asks.

"You have to at least slow it down." Wil points at the crate and the sled. "Otherwise, it'll hit too hard and likely blow out the grav-sled."

Maxim groans and takes his place. "Ok, Zephyr, I'm ready." He can see the crate above, seemingly floating over the railing. It falls right at him. He grunts and sags below the weight of the crate as he catches it. Turning, he slides it—not quietly, but that doesn't matter now—into the larger crate.

"I'm coming down," Zephyr says, before there's a thud on the grating. Wil sees two of the guards spin in his direction, probably feeling Zephyr's landing through their boots.

Knowing she's somewhere around him, he asks, "Will you fit in there? I think it'll be easier if we don't have to worry about you."

The grav-sled bobs a little then settles. "It's tight, but I'm good. Close it up."

Wil watches Maxim shut the lid to their crate and seal it like it was never open. "Bennie, you almost ready?"

"Okay, I'm ready when you are. Everything will come back online together, so be ready," the hacker warns. He's either excited or nervous, his voice a bit higher-pitched than normal.

Wil looks at Maxim, who nods and removes his goggles, and then jogs over about ten paces from the grav-sled. "Do it."

Immediately, the vault doors snap shut, the lights come back on, the life support system is up and running, and all four guards are flailing, pulling their helmets off, shouting—even Helpful Guard, who had stood stock still until now.

Wil turns toward Helpful Guard, putting on his best frantic expression. "What the hell was that?! What happened? Are we under some kind of attack?!" he yells.

Angry Guard interrupts him. "What do you mean? You did this!" The guard's rifle is pointed right at Wil's face. Helpful Guard also has his rifle up.

"The hell you talking about?" Wil shouts back. "We didn't do dren! We were about to enter my boss's vault, and all hell breaks loose—how is this our fault?" He looks at Maxim, who just shrugs and looks all around.

"You know what, you can grolack yourself, we're out of here! Our boss can send another team, I don't care, but something ain't right here—and I'm not leaving this crate here, to get stolen, or vanished, or whatever the hell just happened here. No thank *you*, not worth my life." Wil motions to Maxim, who turns the grav-sled back to the lift leading to the docking area. "Come on!" he shouts, mid-stride.

"Wait a second." It's Helpful Guard. "I don't know if you should leave until we figure out what happened."

Angry Guard seizes on this. "Exactly, you sit tight! No one leaves until we know what happened!" He and Helpful walk over to the guard kiosk, where they're joined by their other two colleagues. They huddle over the computer terminals for a bit, arguing, but too low for Wil to make out what they're saying. Probably afraid of a repeat incident, none of them have put their helmets back on.

Helpful Guard, who turns out to be a young Palorian—Wil guesses they all don't become Peacekeepers—comes over. "You're free to go. We don't know what happened." He looks around, "And we're not telling anyone about it, since there's nothing to back us up on the computer. You do what you have to do with your boss, but there's nothing to back it up."

"What do you mean you don't know?" Wil is laying it on thick. "The lights went out, I think the life support system shut down, and there was a bunch of loud noises!" He's waving his arms, which usually helps distract people.

"We don't know, there are no logs of anything at all happening, so as far as we're concerned, nothing happened." The guard's face is emotionless; Wil sees he's a pro, maybe ex-Peacekeeper. "I'll escort you back to your ship."

Wil turns and motions for Maxim to follow. He knows the guard will feel better if they're escorted out, and knows too that if he's as freaked out as he's pretending to be, he'd welcome the escort. He nods to the guard, and the trio walk to the lift.

It takes less than thirty seconds to get to the docking section. As they descend, Wil hopes Bennie isn't anywhere to be seen.

When the doors open, Wil and Maxim step out. Helpful Guard follows, looking all around, scanning the room. *Definitely a pro*, Wil thinks.

"Well, have a good journey back to where ever you came from." One last scan of the room and the guard steps back into the lift, but the doors don't close. He's waiting for them to enter the airlock corridor.

Wil and Maxim walk to the airlock corridor. "Well, this was a mission for the books," he says loudly. "No one's gonna believe this one!" He slaps Maxim on the shoulder as they enter the corridor, and turn the corner to the *Ghost*'s airlock. Behind them, he hears the faint whisper of lift doors closing. He finally exhales.

CHAPTER 8

DEPARTURE

As soon as they close up the airlock, Wil and Maxim hurry to the armory/prep area. Wil tilts his head up to address the ship. "Computer, we're back. Begin pre-flight diagnostics."

"Sure thing, captain," the ship's voice chirps.

Wil looks at Maxim. "Still not used to that." He pats the big man on the shoulder, smiling. "We did it."

Suddenly, the crate in the corner starts to thud from inside.

"Oh dren, Zephyr!" Maxim rushes over and unseals the lid. Zephyr, back to being visible, jumps out.

"Did you forget about me?!" she growls, looking at them.

"No!" both answer at the same time, blushing slightly. To avoid her, they start changing out of their outfits, Wil removing one sidearm and some of the armor components from his long coat. "I'll be on the bridge; we should get on our way ASAP."

Maxim had changed from one bland uniform to a slightly less dull jumpsuit, which has become his shipboard uniform. "Aye sap?"

Shaking his head, Wil walks out of the staging room and toward the bridge.

Zephyr begins to strip down out of her Peacekeeper armor, taking each piece off and assembling it on a rack for storage. Shaking her head she mutters, "Humans."

On the bridge, Bennie is at his station. "We're all set."

Wil takes a seat at his pilot station. "Great. Computer, open a comm channel, voice-only, to the station." There's a low beep, indicating the channel is now open. "Station, the Serenity ready to depart."

There's no response from the station, but through the hull, the loud clank of a releasing docking collar can be heard. The view on the main display lurches slightly as the ship drifts away from the docking collar.

Bennie snickers. "Guess they're glad to see us on our way."

Wil eases the ship away from the station and brings her about. Once they are safely distant from the station, he fires the main sublight engines. Keeping his speed to a calm-looking pace is tough, but shooting out like a bat out of hell would be suspicious, and part of this plan hinges on Wil and the crew of the *Ghost*—and the *Ghost* itself—being just a ship and crew, nothing much to recall.

Maxim and Zephyr walk through the hatch and take their stations. Zephyr turns to Wil. "Where to now?"

Wil works the controls for a few beats, then replies, "We're heading to Malkor. Fury would be too hot, even if you three hadn't caused a stir there. It'd be the first place anyone who catches on to this little heist would look. Xarrix has an operation on Malkor and said we could make the delivery there, get paid, and be on our way. On the upside, we don't even have to deal with Xarrix, which believe me is a plus."

Bennie nods his head vigorously. "Yeah, Fury'd be hot, and Xarrix is a scum lord. The gray market on Malkor will have all kinds of tech. Can't wait!"

Wil turns back to his station, as the ship starts the jump to FTL. "Three days FTL, folks—time to relax. I'm getting a grum." He stands and heads for the bridge hatch. "Who's with me?"

A little while later, sitting around the table in the small galley area, the crew are happily exchanging stories about their parts in the heist. For the first time since taking possession of the *Ghost*, Wil feels like the ship is more complete—he feels more complete. The fear of being alone in space for the rest of his life is finally starting to fade.

Wil smiles. The funk he'd been feeling and fighting off has diminished slightly.

Maxim is relating how hard it was to stay silent the entire time, when Bennie interrupts: "You hardly ever talk, suddenly you wanted to get chatty?" Everyone laughs, including Maxim. Wil smiles.

Zephyr takes a long swig of her grum. "You both had it easy! I had to jump off that railing, catch myself and hang there, all without making a single sound!" She mimics holding herself on the railing, while Maxim nods and grins at her. "You know the suit makes me nearly invisible, not soundproof!"

"We're lucky I wasn't doing your part—you know I'm no good at the silent stuff, special armor or not," Maxim replies.

Wil laughs. "Yeah no offense pal, but you are not the limber gymnast type." Bennie guffaws, a loud high-pitched braying laugh. Everyone turns.

He stops. "What, that was funny! Now I'm picturing Maxim in some type of gymnastics outfit, prancing around." A punch in this tiny arm ends that mental image. Maxim grins.

Zephyr takes in the scene, and looks the group, then at Wil. She asks the question they've all been wanting to ask. "So, what's in the crate?"

"Coming to you live from Studio Seven at GNO, I'm Mon-el Furash. Reports are beginning to trickle in of a conflict in the unaffiliated system of Harrith. A rebel group has—apparently out of nowhere—

risen up and is demanding... well, many things, with sovereignty for one of the moons in the system being the primary goal, it would appear. It's unclear if this rebel group is new, or merely an escalation of an existing issue in the Harrith system." The newscaster, a heavyset female Malkorite, is reporting from behind a desk at GNO, the Galactic News Outlet. "As viewers may know, Harrith is located near the outer frontier of the Galactic Commonwealth, and, while not an official member, does engage in trade with many of its neighbors, who are GC members. Until recently, there have been no reports, official or otherwise, of trouble in this remote system—but something has changed. It seem these rebels are now well armed, and well equipped." She looks off screen, then back. "I'll keep you posted as things develop out on the frontier. I'm Mon-El Furash, and good day."

WHAT'S IN THE CRATE?

The crew is standing around the crate, now placed in the middle of the cargo hold.

Wil looks at each of them. "You know we shouldn't be opening this, right?"

Bennie looks up from where he's kneeling next to the crate's control panel. "Did Xarrix explicitly say not to open it?"

Wil sighs, "No, he didn't. He also didn't say 'go ahead and rummage through the thing I'm paying you to steal' either, so you know, maybe don't."

Maxim chips in: "Then it's settled, we open it. I think it's only fair to see what we risked our lives for. Also, I'm bigger than you."

Wil shrugs. "Fine. Bennie, can you open it? Ideally so that we can close it back up, and there's no evidence we touched it."

Bennie scrunches up his face, in what is presumably a look of indignation among Brailack. "I just hacked an entire space station—a super secure, secret space station, including the armor suits of the guards. You know what, though? This shipping crate might be too good. I might not be able to crack it." He shrugs.

Wil kicks him. "Don't be a dick."

Bennie rubs his leg. "So undervalued." He plugs his wrist comm into the data port on the crate.

Two seconds later, with a hiss, the crate opens. The lid slowly lifts up and away from the top.

Bennie backs up, trying to look inside. "What's in it? What's in it?"

Wil, Zephyr, and Maxim look up from the crate to Bennie. Together, all three say, "A robot."

Inside the crate, is a matte black robot, curled into a fetal position. That is the only way it would fit inside the crate, its legs are long and thin. It must stand just over two meters. The entire thing is black, except it's joints, which are the dull gray color of whatever material the thing is made out of.

Bennie waves his arms and nearly screams. "COOL!" He takes a running leap and lands on the edge of the crate to look down into it. "Can we keep it?!" He looks up at Wil.

"No! No, we can't keep it! Close the lid. We saw what was in the box." Wil stalks out of the cargo hold.

"What's wrong with him?" Maxim asks.

Zephyr shrugs. "Who knows." She looks down at the form inside the crate. "What do you make of this?"

Maxim frowns. "Looks like a service bot of some type, definitely upgraded. Look here—that's not standard." He points at a module welded to the bot's shoulder, the only other thing on it that isn't matte black. "Wonder why it's in a crate?"

"And why it's so valuable," Zephyr adds. "And what *that* thing does." She too looks at the shoulder attachment.

Bennie looks at the two Palorians, "Let's find out." He reaches in and activates the robot.

All three take a step back. The bot inside the crate begins to make noises: faint whirs, and clicks. Slowly, it stands up inside the crate. Its featureless face rotates to each of them in turn, yellow optical sensors spinning and focusing. Once standing, it's just over two meters tall, with long thin arms and legs, and a sleek but boxy body, a mix of angles and curves. The head is roughly oval-shaped, but the only features are the eyes—nothing else. Most bots the team have seen look distinctly more biological, presumably to help make their owners and operators more comfortable. This one was clearly not designed that way. There are two shorter arms tucked up against its body, perhaps for more fine motor control than the larger arms and hands are capable of.

"Hello." It again turns to face each of them, one at a time. "I am engineering service bot GBE-102002." Its voice is neutral and largely genderless, slightly deeper than Zephyr's voice. "Where am I? Who are you? I am not detecting any Peacekeeper comms; I am no longer on a Peacekeeper vessel." This is not a question, more statement of fact.

GABE

"What part of 'no' wasn't clear?" Wil is furious and pacing the common area, while the crew sits in silence. GBE-102002 is standing in the corner of the galley, head tracking Wil as he paces the small space. "I didn't not answer. I didn't give you a vague answer. I *very clearly* said 'no' when I left the hold."

Bennie looks at Wil. "Technically, you said we couldn't keep it, not that we couldn't turn it on."

Wil grabs a pillow off the chair next to him and hurls it at Bennie, who yelps and just barely avoids a pillow to the face. "Why would you think it was okay to turn it on if we weren't keeping it? What if it was some kind of killbot, or something?"

The robot raises one hand. "Excuse me, but I am not a killbot. For what it is worth. Also, if it helps, you may use male pronouns when speaking about me. I have found selecting one gender or another helps biological beings more easily interact with me." The robot's voice is oddly accent-less, and could easily be a low pitched feminine voice, or a slightly high baritone. If you weren't looking at a robot it would be nearly impossible to tell the gender or race that belongs to the voice.

"Not talking to you!" Wil yells, not even turning around. "Now we have to turn it off and get it back in the crate. Xarrix is waiting for our delivery, or at least one of his goons on Malkor is. We need the money—that gear Zephyr and Maxim bought wasn't cheap. Bennie needs gear, too. We can't stiff Xarrix on this. Even if we didn't need the credits, stiffing Xarrix isn't a good idea."

Zephyr sets down her cup of coffee. "Do we know if Xarrix knows what he's waiting for?" She turns to the robot. "GBE-10022, do you know why you were in the crate? Do you know what modifications have been done to you?"

"First, to be clear, my designation is GBE-102002. Since awakening, I have been running every diagnostic I possess. All that I can say is that I am fully operational. I was designed to work aboard larger vessels in an engineering capacity. The modifications you ask about, however, are a mystery to me." It reaches back and touches the piece of equipment welded to its back and shoulder. "This device is a mystery. It is integrated into my power systems, yet all of its functions are firewalled from my primary systems. I can also identify an encrypted block of data in my central databank that I do not possess the key for."

Maxim looks thoughtful. "Xarrix must want that data, or whatever your add-on does—or both."

"I do not know this Xarrix. My previous place of work was the Peacekeeper Carrier *Pax Magellanic*, in the primary engineering space. I reported to Lieutenant Ablex."

Zephyr and Maxim both look aghast. "You're a *Peacekeeper* bot?" they ask in unison. Zephyr looks at Wil. "Do you think this could be related to why we were framed?"

Wil collapses down into the nearest chair. "Fuck, I don't know. Maybe. Certainly seems like a weird coincidence otherwise. Damn it, I *knew* this wasn't going to be easy. Nothing with Xarrix is ever easy. What's he gotten me tangled up in? Hell, what's he gotten himself tangled up in? Why's he trafficking in stolen bots?"

Bennie stands up. "look. I know you don't think we should have turned it on, but obviously that ship has gone FTL. So why don't we figure out what's going on? We're still a few days out from Malkor. I can dig around in BGE-8675309's databanks, maybe decrypt the data block, or break the firewalls on his additional hardware. Worst case: I can't. Best case: we know more when we get there and can make better decisions." Bennie spreads his hands wide. "Come on, you know you're curious." He smiles, which is slightly off-putting, given all those pointy teeth.

The bot raises its hand. "Excuse me. It is GBE-102002."

"Okay, okay. Fine, GBE... I can't keep saying all that. Gabe, Gabe is your name. Would you mind going with Bennie to engineering, Gabe?"

"Thanks, Wil." Bennie heads for the hatch, and Gabe turns to follow.

"Don't thank me yet. We're in deep shit here, you guys. I can't emphasize this enough." Wil sighs and stands up, heading to the galley and food storage area. "I need a damn grum."

For Wil, the last week has been both the most exciting of his life and complete hell. The *Reaper* is still sitting at the spaceport on Gupta, its crew coming and going, while some type of cargo is being loaded onto the ship. Wil has had some freedom to move around the ship, but Lanksham has made it clear he wasn't to leave the *Reaper*, so the closest he's gotten to this alien planet they're on is looking at the tarmac from the upper level of the cargo area—which is not much of a view. The *Reaper* doesn't have any windows, which seems like a major design flaw to Wil.

Space is limited on the ship, so Wil's been assigned a small closet with a bed in it. Thankfully, he's not bunking with anyone else, which is a minor plus based on what he's overheard from the rest of the crew. Jax and Rolo, the two goons he met on his first day, are apparently an item, but bicker more than any married couple Wil has ever met. Luckily, his bunk—such as it is—isn't near their shared quarters. Apparently when they make up, it keeps their neighbors up.

Lanksham hasn't given him a role yet, so Wil's mostly a cabin boy, which—while cool and exciting in kid's books—actually sucks, at least when the pirates are space pirates. The crew lounge makes the worst hostel in the Third World look luxurious by comparison, and it's Wil's job to keep it clean, which apparently is a source of great amusement for the crew, who seem hell bent on doing their best to destroy the place on a daily basis.

He's scrubbing something off the table when Lanksham enters. "Wil, come with me." Without another word, the captain turns and heads back out of the lounge area.

Wil drops his sponge and follows the tall alien. "What's up?" he asks, catching up with Lanksham halfway to the bridge.

The captain slows down and looks at Wil. "We're done here on Gupta. The last of the cargo is here and being loaded now. Rolo and Jax are seeing to getting it stored."

Wil nods. "Okay, cool." *Why am I being told this?*

"It's time for you to decide what you're going to do." Lanksham looks Wil in the eyes. "You can stay here on Gupta, find work. There are plenty of opportunities."

Wil looks down at his hands. There's grime and whatever that was on the table on them. "I don't want to leave the ship. I don't know you any better than I did a week ago, and I know more about Jax and Rolo than I ever wanted to... but now that I'm stuck out here, in space, and can never go home, I want to see it all."

Lanksham smiles. "I thought you might say that. Good to hear. This planet sucks, but I wanted it to be your choice. Be clear: this isn't a cruise ship. If you're crew, you work. We do what we need to, to keep flying. We don't do always do nice things."

Wil isn't entirely sure what that means, but knows this ship, its crew, and its captain are all part of some kind of space piracy. "I understand."

Lanksham smiles. "I doubt it—but you will, eventually." He continues toward the bridge. "The crew lounge isn't going to clean itself."

Wil is sitting in the lounge he's just cleaned when Rolo-- the taller of the two aliens—enters. "Hey tiny creature, this place looks nice."

Wil lifts his grum in a toast. "Thanks, Rolo. Where's Jax?"

The big alien—Wil still doesn't know what his race is called—plops down into the seat next to Wil. "Finishing up in the cargo hold. The last load is bigger than Lanksham planned. It's taking some extra work to get it all to fit. Jax's okay—he's great with making things fit. Grab me one of those."

Wil grunts, swallowing the reply on the tip of his tongue. He gets up and grabs a grum from the kitchenette, tossing it to—or at—Rolo, who snatches it out of the air with one clawed hand. Wil falls back into his seat. "So where are we going next? Where's the cargo going? What *is* the cargo, for that matter?"

Rolo looks at him. "None of your business, none of your business, and, none of your business."

Just then, Jax walks in. Rolo stands up. "Everything good to go?"

The less large of the pair grabs the bottle of grum and takes a gulp. "Yeah, we're good. I let Lanksham know." The two walk over to the kitchen table.

Wil is still sitting in his chair when the small green alien who hacked his pod comes in. Apparently, his species is called Brailack. "Hey, Pink-skin. What're you doing?"

"What's it look like, Ulgo? Sitting here, enjoying a grum after cleaning this lounge after you filthy animals destroyed it. Again." Wil raises his bottle. "Say, you know where we're headed? Tweedledee and Tweedledumb won't tell me."

The annoying Brailack barks out a laugh. "We're going to Zel'yr. I don't think you want to know what the cargo is, but trust me when I say, Zel'yr isn't a friendly place. I think Lanksham took this job so we'd have a few more credits in the ship's accounts."

"Do we need the money?"

"Who doesn't need money?"

"Huh, I guess. But if it's that dangerous..."

"You worry like this all the time Pinky?" The small hacker is leering at Wil.

"You know, I'm literally twice as tall, and... mmm, probably three times as strong as you. Right?" He reaches over and punches Ulgo.

PART THREE

CHAPTER 9

SECRETS

In engineering space, the banks of equipment blink steadily. "Come on, sit over there." Bennie points to a spot on one of the small workbenches.

"Very well," the bot says, sitting down on the slightly-too-small bench. Its small secondary arms twitch slightly, fidgeting.

Bennie starts getting things ready. "So you know where you used to work, but don't recall why you were in the crate or what led to your being in the crate? Or how you got off your ship?"

"I am afraid that is correct. I do not. The last thing I remember.... The last thing I remember is... The last thing..." The bot tilts its head. "I do not know the last thing I remember. There is apparently a large segment of corrupted memory blocks. The corruption is near the encrypted blocks. That is interesting."

Bennie reaches out to access the front panel on Gabe's torso. "You're telling me!"

Gabe's head tilts. "Telling you what?"

Bennie shakes his head. "Well, you obviously have a secret. Those are always exciting, but it sure looks like you're connected to whatever Maxim and Zephyr found out about the Peacekeepers and their plans to mess everything up in the sector so they can make more money and take over. Grolacking Krebnacks, I hate Peacekeepers." He jumps up and down. "So! Exciting!"

"Why do you hate the Peacekeepers? They serve a noble purpose, dedicating most of their population to helping keep order in the galaxy." Gabe looks down at Bennie, who is now attaching data cables to the open access panel on its chest. The terminal on the bench next to Gabe begins displaying diagnostic data.

"That's what they want you to think. The reality is they're bullies who've tricked the sector into thinking they're this wonderful organization that keeps everyone safe. Except they extort those that don't pay up directly, and they stomp all over everyone's privacy with no consideration whatsoever. They keep technology for themselves, so they always have an advantage. Plus they do the bidding of the Tarsi first, above all else." Bennie walks over to the terminal, still talking. "They've destroyed entire colonies and not paid for it. They fake crimes so that they can kidnap people to feed their war machine. There are even rumors that the war with the Confederacy of Trib was started by the Peacekeepers, to demonstrate their value before that last tax increase the Tarsi rolled out. Now, from what Zephyr and Maxim say, they're doing it again—or at least trying. Krebnacks."

"I had no idea. The engineers I worked with seemed so nice." Gabe turns to look at Bennie, his optic sensors spinning to focus on the small hacker. "Are you and the crew going to stop them?"

Bennie looks up. "Beats me. I just met these drennogs—well, the two Peacekeeper ones at least. I've known Wil since he got the *Ghost*. He doesn't seem to want to get involved, and I can't blame him. You don't last long out here fighting fights that aren't yours. It's the fastest way to suck vacuum. Or blaster barrel? Whichever is worse."

"Both sound like bad things."

Bennie looks at his terminal. "Okay, let's see if I can't help you get your memories back, and maybe see what that doodad on your shoulder is." He watches the data scrolling by for a moment, frowning. "What the..?"

Gabe turns its head. "What did you find?"

"Someone dug around in your data banks and encrypted a day or so's worth of data. Immensely poorly, I might add. They botched it up real good. Like, they just took a chunk of memory and encrypted it in place, not bothering to copy it to another location or anything. No wonder you're having trouble."

"Can you effect the needed repairs?"

Bennie looks over at Gabe. "I won't take offense at that, since we just met."

"Thank you. I think." Gabe turns and stares at nothing.

Bennie continues to work for a few minutes, whistling a tune that's presumably popular on Brailack. "There we go!" He looks over at Gabe. "I need to put you in sleep mode so that I can access the data. I think that's what they did wrong in the first place, messing with your memories while you were online. When I wake you up, everything should be integrated properly."

"Very well," Gabe says. "Entering power save mode." His optic sensors go dark and his head droops forward.

"This is some grolacked dren right here," Bennie says to himself. He reached for the comms panel on the wall. "Hey everyone, get down here." He gets back to work, furiously tapping commands into the console with one hand, while touching various parts of Gabe's insides with a probe.

A few minutes later, Wil, Zephyr, and Maxim enter the engineering space. "What's up?" Zephyr asks. "You figure out its memory issues?"

"Sure did," Bennie nods. "I just decrypted them and am re-integrating them into his main databank. Once he boots up, he'll have full access to whatever it was they wanted to block out." Bennie looks up from his console. "Ready?"

THE REVEAL

With a few whirs and clicks, Gabe's optic sensors begin to light up. They spin and focus, and then the tall robot looks from face to face, before settling on Wil.

"I remember now," it says. "All of it."

Wil turns and opens the hatch behind them. "Let's go back to the galley. I get the feeling this will warrant some coffee, and maybe popcorn." He leaves the room, and Zephyr follows.

Maxim looks at Bennie. "What's popcorn?"

The hacker looks up at his much taller crewmate. "Beats me. Come on, Gabe."

When they are all seated around the galley table, a cup of coffee in Wil's hands, he says, "Okay, Gabe. Let's hear it."

The tall robot looks around. "Very well.

"As I told you already, I am an engineering bot. I was assigned to the Peacekeeper Carrier *Pax Magellanic*, in the main engineering compartment.

"I was assigned the task of de-ionizing several of the secondary purge systems, located in a smaller sublevel of engineering. It was there that I got into trouble. I was working on the third of my twelve purge valves when I heard voices.

"Usually, I would not have cared about that; conversations took place all day in the engineering spaces. However, these voices weren't any that I had a voice print match for, meaning that they were not part of the engineering crew. As such, they were accessing locations and possibly systems they were not cleared to access.

"One of my secondary protocols is to protect the ship, and its crew, to the best of my abilities. If there are saboteurs aboard, it is my duty to stop them. I stopped what I was doing, and went to investigate."

Wil holds up a hand. "Time out." He gets up and refills his cup. "Anyone want some popcorn?" He presses a few buttons on the food processor, and a bag of popcorn plunks out onto the tray. "Sorry Gabe," he says, sitting down again. "Go on." He takes a handful of popcorn, and passes the bag to Maxim.

"As I was..."

"Oh, my gods! This is delicious! Zephyr, try some!" Maxim grabs another handful of popcorn, then passes the bag to his companion. He looks at Wil. "Your planet is full of wonders!"

Wil nods. "Truth."

Zephyr takes a handful and hands the bag to Bennie who also reaches in, but not before licking all his fingers. He moves to hand the bag back to Wil, who waves it away. "Keep it dude, so gross."

Bennie looks around. "What?"

Gabe makes a coughing type noise, or at least what it might sound like if a robot could cough. "As I was saying... I followed the voices through the engineering space. While not as large as the main engineering compartment, secondary engineering spaces on board Peacekeeper carriers are still quite large. I heard the conversation long before reaching the speakers. They were talking of a plan to undermine the governments of four different star systems, sowing dissent through rebellions and encouraging neighbor systems to get involved.

Once one or two of the systems erupted into chaos, the Peacekeepers could come in, stabilize the region, and establish their presence in systems they've been unable to invade legally as yet. It seemed like a rather well-thought-out plan. It occurred to me that perhaps it was best not to confront the perpetrators directly, but rather to report the issue to someone above me.

"Unfortunately, as that thought was processed, I accidentally kicked a pipe that some careless crew member had left laying in the walkway. I reached down to move it safely out of the way, and when I stood up, one of the perpetrators shot me. I assume it was a stunner, since the next time I came online, my diagnostics reported no physical damage, yet I noted a lapse in my internal clock of four tocks."

Zephyr and Maxim look at Wil. "Wil, this is related! This is proof of what we discovered! We can expose the plot!"

Wil raises his hands to quiet the table. "Woah, woah, *woah*. Let's all just take a breath here."

"I am not done with my story. Should I continue, or..?"

The others all fall silent. Wil looks at Gabe. "Yeah, keep going."

"Very good. As I said, when I came back online I was undamaged, except that I could not move. My motor control systems had been disabled. One of the men I had observed plotting was in the room, as was a Peacekeeper ensign. They were discussing disposing of me. The first man was of higher rank, a Commander. The last words the man said to the ensign were, 'Just get rid of the bot, it better not exist by morning,' and then he left. I never saw that man again. Neither person seemed to realize I was back online."

"Oh gods, this is grotesque. What'd they do?" Zephyr is leaning forward, a rather horrified look on her face.

"Thankfully for me, the ensign had other plans. From what I overheard, he owed someone large sums of money, and was able to broker a deal selling me, and the data I contained, to that party."

"Xarrix's competitor, I assume," Wil offers.

"Possibly. The ensign never used a name. All I overheard was the negotiation. The ensign was to trade me, and the data I had recorded about the coup and some modifications... which explains this," he says, touching the modification on his shoulder, "in exchange for the wiping clean of his debt. Shortly after that, the ensign encrypted my databanks, not realizing I was still online. That would explain the degradation." Gabe looks around the room, "The next thing I recall is being activated inside a crate in your cargo hold."

THE DEAL

After two days of FTL, the *Ghost* is entering the Fel-lor system, home of the planet Malkor. Everyone is on the bridge, including Gabe.

"Are you sure about this, Wil? We could turn around, find work... I don't know... somewhere." Zephyr is sitting at her station, looking concerned.

"Yeah, there's no getting around it. If we screw Xarrix, finding work will be next to impossible—at least work that doesn't turn our stomachs. I don't mind bounty hunting, but I'm not getting into cartel work." Wil is at his pilot station, guiding the ship down the gravity well toward Malkor. They are still a good hour out from the planet.

Maxim is at the weapons management console. "Do you think he will accept the deal you plan to offer him?"

Wil shrugs. "I don't know. He's not a complete psychopath or anything, so he can be reasoned with. I've had to negotiate my way out of trouble with him before... but yeah, this is a big one. We don't know what he agreed with to load Gabe up with, and Gabe can't access those systems without the passcodes the ensign is supposed to provide on payment. Payment he isn't going to get now." He shrugs again. "Anyway, here's the plan once we get down there."

Wil looks at each member of his crew.

"Zephyr, you and Bennie are tackling his shopping list." He looks at Bennie. "Yeah, I don't trust you—not one bit, even a little. She'll control the money; you tell her what you need, and sell her on it, and she'll pay. Zephyr, if you think he's bullshitting, don't pay. End of story, Bennie. This job, even if it pays, won't be enough for everything as it is."

He looks at Maxim. "Which brings me to you, Max. Take Gabe and go grocery shopping. I've sent a list to your PADD of things we need, things I'd like to have, and things that would be cool if you can get 'em cheaply."

Gabe, who's standing near the back of the bridge, by the hatch chimes in. "Are you certain it is a good idea for me to leave the ship?"

"Yeah, I think it'll be okay. This will either work or not. Whether you're on the ship or out shopping, it probably won't matter much. You know, things were a lot easier when it was just the *Ghost* and me, and I wasn't almost broke."

Zephyr smiles. "I think I speak for everyone here, when I say we appreciate it. You've given literally all of us a new lease on life." She looks down at her console, which is beeping. "Incoming comms from Malkor space control."

Wil turns to the primary display. "On screen."

The display switches from the stars to a gruff-looking Malkorite female. "Incoming vessel, please identify yourself and state your purpose in this system." She sounds bored.

Wil smiles. "Hi there, Malkor space control, this is the *Millennium Falcon*. We're a small cargo service, here to drop off a crate for a customer, and then look for some work taking us out-system."

The bored Malkorite space control operator looks down at her console, then back up at the screen. "Very well, *Millennium Falcon*, you're clear to approach and land at Gel-nor spaceport, pad... forty-two."

Wil, still smiling. "Gel-nor spaceport, pad forty-two. Roger that, Malkor space control. See you soon."

The space control operator tilts her head; then the screen goes blank.

Wil turns back to Zephyr. "Send that info to the comms account we were given."

"On it."

The *Ghost* weaves its way through the traffic around Malkor, finding a spot in the approach line between two large mass cargo haulers. Thirty minutes later, they're burning through the upper atmosphere. "Switching over to atmospheric engines," Wil says, as the main sub-light engines disengage. There's a moment when everyone's stomach, except Gabe's, lurches slightly, before the boom of the atmospheric engines kicking in, and the press of forward motion returns.

Zel'yr is a binary star system, composed mostly of gas giants. But sitting right in the gravitational sweet spot is Zel'yr Prime. It is a rocky world, covered mainly by ocean. The civilization that originally dwelt on Zel'yr Prime is long since gone, leaving nothing behind but ruins and ghost stories. No one knows what happened to them. They were clearly a technologically-advanced race, but they vanished, their world crumbling to pieces.

Then the Hulgians found it, the perfect world to create a base of operations for a crime syndicate: hard to reach, mostly unknown, and haunted—if you believe in that sort of thing.

The *Reaper* is approaching a space station. Or at least Wil assumes that's what it is—he's never seen one, besides the International Space Station, and compared to that this thing is a freaking *Star Trek* starbase. Lanksham is in his chair. Wil is leaning against the bulkhead by the hatch, and Rolo, Jax, and Ulgo are all at their stations.

"So, who are the Hulgians?" Wil asks.

Jax turns from his station. "Just the most dangerous crime syndicate in the sector. I'd list some of the things they're rumored to be guilty of, but I don't want to give you nightmares."

"No need to be rude." Wil sticks his tongue out.

Lanksham glances back over his shoulder. "Imagine the worst criminals your world has to offer, and multiply that by a hundred. They're involved in everything from slaves and drugs to weapons."

The *Reaper* slides into a large landing bay, next to another ship—only about half as big, but clearly a ship meant for fighting. Wil lets out a low whistle. "That looks mean."

"It's another Ankarran vessel. Earlier model than the *Reaper*, but no less mean. The Hulgians have a fleet of 'em. Even with the Peacekeepers keeping the Ankarrans on a short leash, the Hulgians have quite a few of their best." Lanksham stands, as on the forward display a party is visible walking towards the ship.

The lead Hulgian is a hulking being. Wil can't determine its sex from the screen, but it's huge, and mean-looking. Sort of like a seven-foot-tall triceratops, sans tail. It's not wearing any armor, or weapons that Wil can see, but he supposes that makes sense if this station—and for that matter, the entire planet below—are part of the criminal empire this being runs. Don Corleone didn't wear armor either. Slightly behind and to the right of the massive crime lord is another being, one Wil knows only from the newscasts he's seen on the ship: a Peacekeeper.

"Uh, hey, Lanksham? Isn't that a Peacekeeper?" Wil asks.

"Wil, you stay on the ship." The captain raises his hand to stop Wil's protest. "The Hulgians would exploit your world in a heartbeat, and if they find out I have a Human on my crew, they'll demand I turn you over. That Peacekeeper down there won't help and will likely do what he can to hide the complete enslavement of your people from his superiors and the GC."

"What?" Wil asks. "Enslavement? Why? How?"

The captain looks at him levelly. "Do you really want to find out?"

Wil slumps down in the nearest chair. "Fine."

"There is one thing you can do. Our agreement states that they pay on delivery. The transfer should take place the moment we start moving cargo. Keep an eye on the ship's account. If you don't see the payment, hail me." Lanksham pulls up the account on a secondary display. Wil nods.

Ten minutes later, Wil watches as the number on the ship's accounts increases. He nods to himself—no need to call Lanksham. From the camera in the cargo hold, he can see the captain heading over to the large party, while the crew starts moving crates. Everyone is involved, even the two engineering crew members, who Wil hardly knows.

As the crew offload the cargo, Lanksham and the head Hulgian watch. The Peacekeeper is keeping his distance from them, but not helping with the cargo. Wil takes a seat in Lanksham's chair, looking at them through the various visual feeds from outside the ship. Rolo and Jax are helping to unload, with a few Hulgians pitching in. Ulgo is sitting on a crate watching and—from the look of things—making jokes; Rolo and Jax are trying to stifle laughs, and it seems like one of the Hulgians is too. Everything seems pretty friendly.

Lanksham and the lead Hulgian, meanwhile, are having what looks like a heated discussion. Wil zooms in on the feed; Lanksham looks mad. That mysterious Peacekeeper has moved to stand beside the Hulgian crime boss. Wil hasn't known him long enough to read his expressions, but he looks worried too. Wil pans the view to Ulgo, who's not making jokes now. Rolo and Jax have stopped smiling. All three look anxious, as do the other two crew members at the top of the cargo ramp.

Wil leans forward in the chair. "What the hell is going on?"

Things are looking more and more tense between Lanksham and the lead Hulgian; the other Hulgians are moving away from the crew of the *Reaper*. The Peacekeeper has also stepped away a few paces and is working his wrist comm.

Wil looks up at the ceiling. "Computer, can you identify that Peacekeeper?" A small red square appears over the Peacekeepers head, then flashes and stays green when the alien looks up from his wrist comm.

"Peacekeeper Sub-Centurion Janus," the sexless voice of the ships computer replies. "Commanding officer of the fifth strategic division, first fleet."

Wil reaches for a button on the panel in front of him, to open a comms link to Lanksham and the crew. But before he can press it, all hell breaks loose on the screen. The Hulgians are running all over; the crew is falling to the ground, writhing in pain. Jax has his blaster out, getting off three shots at the Hulgians before falling to the deck.

Wil hits the button. "Lanksham, Rolo! Jax, Ulgo! What's happening?" All he hears from the other end is coughing and gagging. He can see them on screen; they're dying. The Hulgians seem fine though, slowly moving out from behind their cover. Commander Janus is still standing where he was before, smiling, also unaffected. Some type of biological agent then—but how could that be? All six members of the *Reaper*'s crew are dying, but they're all different races. *This doesn't make sense!* "Lanksham! Can you hear me?" *Oh god, what do I do?*

Wil can see Lanksham, writhing on the deck, his hair falling out, his skin turning white. The lead Hulgian is standing right next to him laughing, before saying something Wil can't make out. Ulgo isn't moving at all.

"*Reaper*...." —there's a cough— "Authorization code... Lanksham four three Bravo four four five eight seven." Another fit of coughing, wetter now. "Transfer all command... codes to... crewman... Wil... Wil Calder." Wil sees Lanksham cough up blood. "Emergency proto-col... runaway. Good..." Coughing and gagging. "Good luck, Wil. I'm sorry..." The line doesn't cut out, but Wil doesn't hear anything more, until the lead Hulgian orders his goons into the ship to search it.

"Oh fuck. Oh fuck." On the screen, Lanksham collapses. The others are already dead, or at least not moving. Probably dead—foam is running out of Rolo's mouth. The Hulgians are walking toward the ship. *Oh fuck.* They have their weapons drawn.

Suddenly the ship is rumbling, the cargo ramp is lifting, and the weapons systems are coming online. "What the hell?" Wil says, startled. The lights on the bridge have shifted to a red color, and the station Jax occupied—apparently tactical—has come to life and is running through a list of targets. "Computer, what's happening?"

On the screen, the Hulgians sent to search the *Reaper* are tumbling down the ramp, scrambling away from the ship. Wil has never actually interacted with the computer, but has no choice but to now. On-screen, the ship is lifting off the deck. "Self defense protocols enacted," the voice of the *Reaper* says. "Evasion of capture protocol enacted, Captain."

"Captain?!" The ship is lifting up and spinning to face the opening of the docking bay. Blasters have deployed from the underside of the ship, and are firing at the Hulgians. The shots seem more intent on keeping the Hulgians occupied than harming them. The next thing Wil sees is that the ship has cleared the docking bay. He switches the view aft and sees the Hulgians all standing at the edge of the docking bay; the other Ankarran ship looks like it's powering up.

With no warning, the *Reaper* leaps into FTL.

Wil is standing in the middle of the bridge, looking around, as the stars spin and blur. "Well, shit," he says.

CHAPTER 10

GEL-NOR SPACEPORT

Malkor—and the entire fel-lor system, for that matter—are at best mid-tier as far as population and prestige are concerned. Fel-lor has only two habitable planets. Malkor is the largest. The other, Gilkor is one of the moons orbiting a gas giant. Gilkor is more industrial than its larger cousin: mines, refineries, and so on. Malkor, while boasting a substantial industrial zone, is mostly commercial and residential in nature. Cities that span dozens of kilometers cover the larger continents. The single ocean is covered in small floating towns. While not a major tourist attraction, the planet sees a lot of business and commercial traffic, as well as being a popular stopover for ships and convoys on long-haul, cross-sector trips. In other words, Malkor does alright.

That level of doing 'alright' sometimes leads to ego issues with the elected officials and upper class, who feel their world, and system, are far more important than they truly are. This can result in over-zealous law enforcement of criminal activity.

Which is why Xarrix is not on the planet, but maintains an operation there. While there's no shortage of hoity-toity citizens who like to think crime isn't something their cities and planet have to deal with, there are plenty of others who engage in just about every known vice there is. So Xarrix's operations on Malkor are quite profitable—just a bit risky.

Gel-nor spaceport is situated on reclaimed swampland outside the city of Gel-nor, a mid-sized city for Malkor: several million people contained in a few square kilometers of glass and duracrete. Hundreds of high-rise dwellings create a moderately impressive skyline. If it were the first alien city Wil had ever seen, the skyline would leave him breathless, putting New York, London, Los Angeles and Denver all to shame. Having been on Tarsis, it's only slightly impressive. Having been on Malkor before, it's not even worth a second glance.

Pad forty-two is along the outer ring of landing pads, essentially in the low-rent district. Once the *Ghost* touches down and the atmospheric engines spin down, the cargo doors open and the boarding ramp drops down.

Wil, Zephyr, Maxim, Bennie, and Gabe walk down the ramp, looking round carefully. The spaceport is busy, to say the least: hundreds of ships on the ground, dozens in the air, coming or going. There are thousands of beings from all over the sector going about their business.

"Okay, you all know your jobs. Go get 'em done, then meet back here. Comms me if you have any trouble." Wil lifts his wrist comm. "Computer, lock up the ship—self-defense protocol bravo."

"Acknowledged, captain. Ship is secure."

The spaceport is just outside the city, connected by a wide bridge that houses the first of many shopping districts. Those nearest the spaceport tend to offer the worse selection at the highest prices, since many who land only have a short time on-planet and can't get much further. The experienced spacers walk right through the shopping district, never slowing down to let the buskers get their hands, claws or tentacles on them.

The easiest way to get through the shopping district is to rent a ground car—or, if you're feeling flush, rent a sky car. Wil is feeling neither flush, nor inclined to part with even a single credit he doesn't have to. He heads off in the direction of the nearest pedestrian exit, at least a kilometer away from the *Ghost*.

"We're walking?!" Bennie complains, falling in line with the rest of the crew. "You know my legs are literally half as long as yours? AYE, WHAT THE!?" he screeches as Gabe reaches down and picks him up, depositing him not too gently on its shoulders.

Without missing a step, the robot lifts Bennie's hands off its optic sensors. "Problem solved."

Bennie slaps the top of Gabe's head. "This is embarrassing!"

"Would you rather walk?"

"Carry on, but don't jostle me!" Bennie sniffs, and one hand slips back over the robot's optic sensor.

BENNIE AND ZEPHYR

Arriving at the pedestrian archway of the spaceport, the crew of the *Ghost* comes to a stop to one side, so as not to interrupt the flow of foot traffic.

Wil looks around at them all. "Okay, meet you all back at the *Ghost*. If you get there first, the computer should let you in as long as you have your wrist comm. Gabe, until we get a proper comms unit built into you, you'll have to stick with Maxim to get back onto the ship. If everything goes as planned, I'll only be a few tocks. Zephyr, remember you're in charge of the funds. Don't spend it if you don't have to."

"Does that mean we can steal things?" Bennie chimes in.

Both Wil and Zephyr answer together. "*No.*"

Wil pauses then. "Well... no, you know what. No, no stealing. Too risky."

The rest of the group splits up, heading into the shopping district, leaving only Zephyr and Bennie.

Looking down at Bennie, she extends a hand before them. "Lead the way."

Bennie stalks off down the main walkway of the shopping

district, head up, marching with purpose. Zephyr shakes her head, smiling. It feels good to have friends, even annoying ones.

The walk through the first shopping district takes Zephyr and Bennie some time. As they leave the bridge shopping district, they hit a fork in the main road. Off to one side is a mass of stalls selling clothes, food, and other goods. The other fork leads to the technology sector, as is evident from the neon and holographic buskers.

Bennie makes a kind of cackle-laughing noise, and increases his pace. Zephyr follows.

The small hacker ducks into a shop that clearly sells something electronic, but Zephyr can't tell what that might be. She follows him inside, and sees Bennie deep into a negotiation with the store owner —he had maybe a fifteen tick lead on her, how was he already negotiating?

"This isn't even this year's model multiplexer," he's saying. "Why would I pay the list price?"

"Because it's brand new," the shop owner replies. He's some type of lanky thin being, Zephyr sees, with four arms and not a single hair on its body. Oh, and two tails.

"It's brand new *and* old," Bennie counters. "Take twenty percent off and it's sold."

The shop keeper crosses both sets of arms, uncrosses them, then does this two more times. "Fine, you little monster, twenty percent off. BUT... You also buy your data cables from me."

Bennie smiles. "Deal." He looks over to Zephyr, clearly signalling *pay the being*. She sends over the payment from her wrist comm.

The shopkeeper hands Bennie a bag, and looks at Zephyr. "Thank you."

As they leave the shop, Zephyr looks down at Bennie. "So, what did we just buy?"

Bennie laughs. "A state of the art, albeit last years' model, multiplexer. It's the ..."

She raises a hand. "I won't understand, will I?"

He looks at her, and smiles. "No." He turns and heads deeper into the technology shopping area.

A few stops later, Zephyr has her hands full of bags, a box under each arm, and is looking around frantically. She whistles. "Hey! Cargo bot! Come here."

A cargo bot rolls over, queries Zephyr's wrist comm, then answers. "Hello, the charge for cargo services is one credit per tock. Would you like to pay by the tock or for the entire day?"

Zephyr looks to Bennie. "How much more do you need?"

"How much credit do we have left?" he grins, and rubs his hands together.

Looking at the cargo bot, Zephyr sighs. "We'll pay by the hour. Follow us." She looks at Bennie. "One more stop; make it count."

MAXIM AND GABE

After Wil, Zephyr, and Bennie walk off, Maxim and Gabe look at each other, then head into the nearest shopping district. They take in the sights around them: unlike those closer to the city, this district covers a little of everything, catering to just about any need a traveler with limited time might have—technology, food, clothing, and more, all mixed together. Maxim enjoys markets like this one, compared to the more orderly style closer to the city. This is mostly because he enjoys window shopping, so these kinds of districts give him a little of everything.

Even though his face doesn't show anything, with its two optic sensors, Maxim can't help but feel like the bot is also enjoying the scenery. "Have you ever been to a shopping district before?" he asks. "Or a spaceport, for that matter?"

Gabe turns to look at him. "I have not. Up until this moment, I have never been outside the Peacekeeper Carrier *Pax Magellanic*. More accurately, the engineering spaces aboard that ship. I came online the first time there, and never left."

Maxim shakes his head. "We have much to show you."

They continue walking for a while, Gabe taking in and cataloging everything he sees: every species, every type of food and piece of equipment. He's been online for over fifteen cycles and has never set foot outside the engineering spaces of a Peacekeeper carrier, and he never once gave a single CPU cycle to thinking about leaving. Now, however, watching so many different species all conversing and engaging in commerce, he has a hard time understanding why. There's such wonder in the universe.

Finally, they reach the end of the first shopping district and make their way towards the food stalls. Maxim accesses his wrist comm to check their shopping list. Wil has made notes next to some of the items, presumably indicating acceptable alternatives.

Since Gabe doesn't have the list and has no idea what most of the things on the list are—other than 'food'—he's basically along for the ride. Maxim assumes that Wil simply didn't trust the robot alone on the *Ghost*. If Maxim were in charge, he'd feel the same way. The newest member of their little crew seems pleasant enough, for a bot, but they know only what it's told them of its past life. The fact that it's been modified is also peculiar, and a little worrying. Wil didn't seem to give it much thought, but Maxim knows what kind of Peace-keeper tech can fit in the space available on Gabe's shoulder.

The shopping is slow going. Maxim doesn't know what a lot of the things on the list are, let alone their Wil-approved alternatives. He spends a great deal of time asking shopkeepers for help. Thank-fully, in shopping districts like this one, everyone is friendly, or at least friendly enough. If a vendor isn't going to get your money, they'll help another get it.

At one vendor Gabe looks over Maxim's shoulder at the list. "What is peanut butter?"

Maxim shrugs, "human thing."

WIL

"If everything goes as planned, I'll only be a few tocks," Wil says. "Zephyr, remember you're in charge of the funds, don't spend it if you don't have to."

Without waiting for an answer, he heads off through the shopping district. Glancing at his wrist comm, he makes a connection. "We're on the ground, where are you?"

The screen doesn't show anyone on the other end, but the connection is live. "Chollraw avenue and Axxar Boulevard," says a voice. "'Traxis imports'; ask for Lorath." Then the connection drops.

Wil pulls up the city network, and downloads a map, inputting the intersection he's looking for. *Makes sense it's not too far,* he thinks. The cover business is an importer, and any dealings Xarrix is likely to have would be with people from the spaceport.

He'd get there faster if he took a ground car, but honestly, Wil isn't in a big hurry. Even if Xarrix isn't here, whomever he trusts enough to run his business on Malkor is likely just as bad as Xarrix, and therefore not someone Wil is in a hurry to meet.

So he lets himself enjoy the walk there. The view isn't bad, he has to admit. The corner he's looking for isn't in the fancy part of town, but it's past all the shopping districts, right on the edge of the warehouse district. As such, it's still a vast improvement over the bar Xarrix uses as an office on Fury. It's also apparently the only business on this street, at least the only that's open. There's not a soul anywhere around.

"Great, no witnesses," Wil mumbles.

He walks up to the shop marked Traxis Imports. It's nothing spectacular: a two-story building with a large service door and a smaller personnel door beside it. With one final glance around, he walks in.

The inside of the building is nicer than he expected. The reception desk is wood in a jet black, shot through with gold and silver—the entire desk seems to have been carved from a single piece, from a tree which must have been easily ten feet in diameter. The rest of the room is just as impressive: a sofa made of some animal hide, like leather, though Wil assumes it's not. There's polished metal everywhere, and light seems to come from everywhere and nowhere at the same time, thought he can't see a single light fixture.

The receptionist is, well, beautiful. Wil has never seen her species before. She's humanoid, but with feline accents—whiskers and swishing tail and all.

"Hello, may I help you?" She ends the question with a purring sound.

Wil walks up to the desk and leans on it. He smiles, and gives her a wink. "Here to see Lorath."

"She's expecting you. Is something wrong with your face?" Her smile reveals a set of long sharp incisors. Not waiting for his answer, she continues, "Through those doors." Her tail lifts up and points to a door off to the side.

"Uh, great. Uh, thanks." Wil turns away from the desk, towards the door. "Here goes nothing."

"I'm sorry. What did you say?"

"Nothing." As he approaches the door, it snaps open with a hiss.

"Enter," says a voice from within. If the receptionist's voice was pure sexuality, this voice is pure aggression.

As soon as Wil steps inside the office, the door snaps shut.

"Wil Calder, welcome to Malkor. Do you have Xarrix's merchandise?"

The front office might have been plush, but the back office is downright opulent. That same gold/silver-veined wood is evident here but in the shape of a much larger, much more ornate desk. The room is starkly furnished—just the desk, the being behind it, and two chairs on the other side of the desk. Oh, and there's a giant head on the wall. Wil doesn't know what type of creature it is, but if its teeth are any indicator, it's easily four meters tall and likely vicious.

The being behind the desk is definitely not the same race as the one at the reception desk. She's big, but not bulky, covered in scales that seem to shift from pink to dark purple and back as she moves. Apart from the scales, she's not overly reptilian—almost avian, in fact. She rests her arms on the desk and Wil can see that her powerful arms are in fact wings. At some point, her people could fly. *The galaxy is full of wonders.* This one might try to kill him shortly, but still. He takes a seat opposite Lorath, admiring the view.

Wil reaches out and puts a data chip on the table and slides it across. "Sure do. Here."

She reaches out with one clawed hand, picking up the chip. "This is it? I was under the impression there'd be more to it, like a bot of some type." Her eyes never leave Wil's.

He's about to start into his story when a subtle red light built into the desktop begins blinking. He closes his mouth, looking from the light to Lorath and back. "Uh, what's that?"

Her eyes never leaving his, she stands up. "Stay right there." She walks around the desk, and he sees she's wearing a smart business suit: sleeveless blouse, business-like trousers. She walks to the wall and touches a control. The screen comes to life. On it, Wil catches a glimpse of the front office. The feline receptionist is talking to some-one. *Oh shit.* She's talking to Peacekeepers.

Lorath lets out a hissing sound; she spins and looks at Wil. "You were followed?"

Wil is up and out of his chair. "Are you kidding? Hell no, I wasn't followed! You do something lately that would attract the authorities?"

The look she gives Wil answers that question.

There's a knock at the door. On the screen, the Peacekeepers are standing at the door to Lorath's office.

"Shit." Wil grabs his blaster and reaches to activate his face shield.

The door explodes inward, nearly knocking him over. His face shield comes up just in time, as debris flies everywhere. Two Peacekeepers rush through the remains of the door, blaster rifles at the ready.

One flies backward, as a pulse rifle blast hits him or her squarely in the chest. The other Peacekeeper dives to the side, returning fire. Wil is off to the side crouching, looking around. Lorath has somehow gotten behind her desk, pulse rife in hand, an energy shield sparkling around her. She's taking aim at the other Peacekeeper, as two more storm the doorway, firing in her direction. She ducks behind her desk, taking two hits to her shield. Neither Peacekeeper has seen Wil, so he fires on both of them, distracting them, as Lorath and her rifle take them out.

"We gotta get out of here!" Wil shouts to her, as he runs at a crouch toward her desk.

He stops dead in his tracks as she shifts the pulse rifle to him. "We?"

Wil is about to say something when a grenade rolls into the room. He turns away and dives for the corner, just as the grenade explodes. More blaster fire fills the room. Lorath reaches under her desk. "You're on your own, but this isn't over," she growls. She suddenly drops under the desk, and Wil hears a hatch snap shut.

"Damn it," he hisses, as he makes another dive for the desk. Then he pops back up, firing blindly at the destroyed doorway. "Okay, now what?" he asks himself, dropping down again behind the desk. Blaster bolts are eating away at the ebony wood. The animal head on the wall falls to the floor beside him, scorched from all the weapons' fire.

Before he can formulate a plan, Wil hears a commotion. The blaster fire from the outer room slows, then stops; the yelling, however, increases. He slowly raises his head up, in time to see the immensely-attractive feline receptionist going full ninja warrior on the Peacekeepers. She must have been hiding behind her desk, playing the scared receptionist role until they all turned their backs on her. Wil looks around, trying to think. *Okay, how do I get out of here?* He crawls under the desk; there was a button or something underneath it that she had used. He runs his hands all along the underside of the wood—there it is! He touches the control and the panel under the desk slides away.

The commotion in the outer room is dying down; cat ninja girl has likely been subdued. Wil drops through the open panel into a dark tunnel, and the hatch overhead closes behind him.

"So now what?" Wil asks himself, retracting his face shield, looking around. Then he sees it. "Oh shit."

There's a timer on the wall, counting down. It's almost to zero. Wil reactivates his face shield, along with the night vision mode, and takes off running down the tunnel.

A few meters from what looks like the exit, the entire tunnel erupts in dust, and the whole thing shakes violently. The explosion, Wil realizes, must have leveled the entire building he has just come from.

CHAPTER 11

IT COULD HAVE BEEN WORSE

Maxim and Gabe are the first to return to the *Ghost*. Gabe is loaded down with bags and boxes. As Maxim accesses the ship's systems via his wrist comm, he says, "If nothing else, you saved us the rental fee of a cargo bot." He smiles as the cargo doors open, and the boarding ramp lowers with a hiss.

"Thank you," Gabe answers, from behind a pile of boxes.

"Let's get all this put away, before the others get back."

"Should we secure the ship?" Gabe asks, as they crest the top of the boarding ramp.

"No, the others should be along shortly. Computer, alert us if anyone approaches the boarding ramp."

"Will do," the chipper computer replies from the nearest speaker.

They're almost done stocking the shelves in the pantry when the computer pipes up. "Zephyr and Ben-Ari are approaching the boarding ramp."

Maxim closes the pantry with a clunk. "Thanks." As the other two enter the shared space, Bennie waves to Gabe. "Hey big guy, can you help me unload the cargo bot?"

Maxim walks over to Zephyr, pulling her close. "How was babysitting the small green annoyance?" He leans in and kisses her.

She smiles back. "Surprisingly, not as bad as I expected. Let me tell you about it." They head off to the lounge section, chatting.

Bennie looks up at Gabe. "Did you guys hear the explosion?"

Gabe turns his head toward Bennie, while his arms continue stacking jars of something Wil called 'an ok alternative to Nutella'. He shakes his head. Bennie shrugs.

Just then, there's the sound of the cargo doors closing. "Computer, start the pre-flight procedure," Wil's voice says.

Maxim and Zephyr look up from their conversation. Wil is covered in dust. "How'd it go?" Zephyr asks.

Wil opens the cooler, and grabs a grum. "Well, Xarrix's interests here on Malkor are more or less over. The Peacekeepers raided the place."

Everyone stops what they're doing. Almost in unison, they all say: "What?!"

Wil raises his hand. "Yeah, I know. No idea what the hell happened. I know I wasn't followed, and there's no reason I would be. Lorath must have already been under investigation, and my showing up must have made them jump, thinking I was part of whatever they were up to. Either way, she's flapping in the wind and her building is a lot of rubble, with the parts of a few Peacekeepers thrown in. I gave her the data—I think she had it on her when she fled, but I'm not sure." He looks at Gabe. "For better or worse, you're with us now."

The bot looks at each of them, then turns to Wil. "That is good."

Wil stares back, and blinks a few times. "Alrighty then. I kind of expected more. Anyhoo... let's get the hell out of here."

Zephyr raises her hand. "Uh, what exactly are we going to do now?"

"Oh, yeah, well. I guess we should decide that, huh?"

Maxim clears his throat. "We should take our evidence to the Galactic Commonwealth. Whether Xarrix has that data or not, from what you say about him he wouldn't do the right thing with it."

Wil nods. "My guess is he was hoping to sell it back to the bad guys."

Bennie shakes his head. "We should just hack into one of the main broadcast stations, and transmit the evidence, everywhere."

Zephyr looks at Wil, hard. "We can't do nothing."

Wil looks over at Gabe. "Anything from you? Taking all opinions here."

Gabe tilts his head. "I am just happy to be here."

As if on cue, the ship chimes in. "Captain, the pre-flight checks are complete. We're ready to take off."

COMPLICATIONS

"This just in. We're receiving word that the conflict in the Harrith system has escalated. What was once viewed as a small conflict between two rival factions within the system has since spilled out into neighboring star systems, precipitated by the destruction of a Zengar cargo convoy. The Zengar, until now, have not been involved in the conflict within the Harrith system. The Galactic Commonwealth has not commented on the matter yet, beyond saying that they're closely monitoring the situation. However, observers have noted that several Peacekeeper carriers have begun moving in the direction of the Harrith system, even though the GC and Peacekeepers have no jurisdiction there. The Zengar are dues-paying members of the Commonwealth. It's unclear at this moment whether they have officially requested aid or not. We'll have more as the situation develops. I'm Mon-el Furash, with GNO."

After the broadcast, the display returns to the view of stars.

Wil breaks the silence. "Well, fuck."

Zephyr stands up at her station. "We have to do something."

Wil sighs. "I know, I know. Damnit." Running both hands through his hair, he groans. "We have to go to Harrith."

Gabe, who has taken up a spot standing by the hatch, asks, "Is that wise? Based on the newscast we just saw, the Harrith system is likely to be quite dangerous."

"Would it make more sense to go to Zengar," Maxim chimes in. "Or maybe even Tarsis directly?"

"No," Zephyr replies. "I think Wil is right. It has to be Harrith. Showing them the proof we have will immediately discredit the Peacekeepers, and the rebels will probably lose all public support. They likely have support right now because no one knows the Peacekeepers are supplying them. Dren, the rebels may not even know who's supplying them."

Wil looks down at his console. "Setting course for the Harrith system. It's the only play that makes sense, and honestly, the only play that I can see where we have a chance of not dying. Gabe, get down to engineering. It's been a few years since the *Ghost* has had a proper engineer aboard—do whatever you need to do to get things shipshape down there. Now that you're connected to the ship's network, just send over a list of must-have parts."

"Yes, Captain." Gabe turns to the hatch.

Wil nods at the departing bot, then turns to Maxim. "You might still get your shot with those weapons. Run all the diagnostics, get everything ready, and make a list of anything you need. Must-have's only."

Bennie sits up at his station. "Can I go shopping again?!"

"No!" Wil snaps, holding up a finger. "But you can get ready. We're gonna need new ship IDs and transponder codes—at least two: one to get us into the area, another to get us out. To be safe, maybe one or two more. Plus, if you can work on those firewalls on Gabe's backpack, that'd be great."

"You know how hard it is coming up with clean names and codes that pass even a little bit of investigation, let alone Peacekeeper levels?" Bennie asks. "That's no small ask; it'll take me days, at the very least."

"I know. Time to put all that gear I bought you to work, and you better get started." Wil turns to Zephyr. "This isn't going to be easy."

She smiles. "But it'll be worth it. ETA?"

Wil looks down at his console. "A week—probably a little longer if we have to make a stop to pick up essentials. Computer, keep tabs on GNO and other news sources for mentions of the Harrith system, or the Zengar system."

"Of course, Captain," the computer replies brightly.

Within two days, the *Ghost* is entering orbit over Trull Prime.

***

The crew stands on the bridge, watching the planet spin below them as they begin their descent to the surface. Gabe and Maxim both have shopping lists that make Wil's head spin, even after being pared down to what he considers the essentials. The report from engineering was worse than the one from tactical, which Wil had expected. He's had more occasion to use the ship's weapons and knows what works and what doesn't—though in his years of owning the *Ghost*, he's never used all the available weapons. The missile bay is nearly empty, the port side disrupter emitter is in need of replacement, and the targeting computer is two firmware releases behind. *That explains some of my targeting issues in the past,* Wil thinks, remembering a time when some pirates were chasing him and the computer couldn't seem to hit a damn thing. *I just hope we don't have to try to shoot anything.*

The *Reaper* has been flying in FTL for somewhere around twelve hours. Wil has been sitting silently on the bridge the entire time. The images of his... well, technically captors, but also friends, sort of... dying horrible deaths at that space station have been repeating over and over in his mind. Lanksham, bloody foam spilling from his mouth at the feet of the lead Hulgian. Rolo and Jax collapsed near the grav-sled with crates loaded on it. Ulgo lying on the crate he'd been sitting on, blood pooling around his head. Lanksham's last words over the comms unit: 'Good luck, Wil. I'm sorry.'

"You're sorry? You're sorry?" he mumbles. His voice is scratchy from lack of use.

The bridge is dark. It's night on board the ship, and even though Wil has been mostly catatonic the last twelve hours, the *Reaper* has been carrying out its final orders: 'runaway.' To where Wil has no idea. The ship jumped to FTL, and he hasn't moved or spoken since.

"Computer?" he croaks. "What's. What's our destination?"

"Current destination is spatial coordinates..." The computer rattles off a string of numbers that have no meaning to Wil.

"Computer, stop. Take us out of FTL."

The primary display shifts back, from stretched-out star lines to thousands of little points of light.

"Computer, are there any ships near us? Or planets?"

There's a slight pause, as the computer consults the sensor data. "Negative," the emotionless response comes from the overhead speakers. "There are no ships within sensor range. There are no planets or star systems within sensor range."

Wil stands up, his legs sore from not moving in hours. Suddenly he realizes he has to pee! A few minutes later, he's back on the flight deck, looking over each station, remembering the being who last sat there. He had barely known them, had only been part of the crew a few weeks, but he had come to terms with the fact that he was never going home, and that for better or worse the *Reaper* was his home... but now—now what? Can he operate the ship on his own? Does he want to? What would he do with it? Maybe sell it, and get something else, something more suited to his nature? He doesn't even know what the ship is worth.

He spends a week drifting in deep space, cleaning. The ship was always dirtier than he could stand, but with six aliens doing their best to dirty it and one trying to clean it, he had never stood a chance.

The cleaning helps keep his mind off his situation. Every new station or section he moves on to, he asks the computer for an overview of its function and level of automation, building a mental list of what running the ship solo might look like.

After the ship is as spotless as he can get it, he returns to the bridge and looks around. "I can't avoid this any longer, can I?"

"Please restate the question," the computer replies.

"Not talking to you. Wait—actually I am. Put a star map up on the main display, the *Reaper* in the center, and highlight planets with spaceports we can afford to land at." The main screen switches to a zoomed-out view spanning several light years, with the ship in the center. A half-dozen planets are highlighted, their names on a tag next to each.

Wil walks around the forward stations, right up to the main

display. Humming to himself, he leans toward the screen. "Mmmm, Fury."

He walks back to the central control station, where Lanksham had piloted the ship from. "Computer, set a course for Fury, and take us to FTL."

The display reverts to its normal view and the stars stretch into lines. "Computer, ETA Fury?"

A beep, then, "Four standard days."

Nodding, mostly to himself—since the computer, as far as he knows, can't see him—he says, "Computer, does the ship have any type of training mode so I can get up to speed on piloting it?"

"Affirmative, this vessel is equipped with a training simulation mode. This mode can be activated while travel is underway."

Wil plops into the captain's seat—*my seat now, I guess*—and tells the computer, "Okay, activate training simulation. Wait. Do you have other voices?"

"There are a number of voice prompts available. Would you like them listed?"

After spending nearly fifteen minutes listening to the ship say the same thing over and over in different languages and sexes (or lack thereof), Wil picks one.

Turning to face the main display, he says clearly, "Okay, now let's go ahead and start the simulation mode." Then to himself, he adds, "you've got four days, Calder, let's do this."

"Simulation commencing," the new bland, but clearly male, voice responds.

PART FOUR

CHAPTER 12

JUST THE ESSENTIALS

Trull Prime lies halfway between Malkor and the Harrith system, as good a place as any to stop and do some shopping. The black market there is thriving, which is a good thing since that's where Maxim's shopping list will take them. Gabe's shopping list is easier and more straightforward, and considerably shorter.

As they cruise through the clouds over Trull Prime, atmospheric engines roaring, Wil addresses the team. "Okay guys, here's the deal. We're scraping the bottom of the ship's accounts again. Lorath didn't get around to paying—not that she necessarily would have anyway. I doubt anyone is gonna be handing out credits in the Harrith system, so bargain hard—bargain like your life depends on it, because it might, if we can't get some credits in the account after this. Gabe, you take Bennie—according to Zephyr, he's a born negotiator." Wil nods to the Brailack, who's beaming. "Zephyr, Maxim and I will hit the night market, and get the weapons and parts to repair the ship's tactical systems. Questions?"

No one says a thing.

"Good. Then let's do this—faster we're done, faster we're on our way to Harrith." Everyone nods. "You know, I sprung you two, thinking it was just a jab at the Peacekeepers. Now I'm thinking karma is a bitch."

Gabe leans forward from his spot by the door. "Who is Karma?"

The spaceport they touch down in is one of the larger ports on the planet. Wil has already identified the night market where they can get their weapons system components. The *Ghost* may be more or less legitimately owned, but that doesn't change that fact that munitions of the type she uses are hard for non-military personnel to get their hands on. The night market is their best bet—home to just about everything a being could want, from drugs, weapons, technology, sex, and slaves, to things beyond normal comprehension. Wil rarely visits night markets. For one thing, going alone is a dangerous proposition. For another, they're so full of things Wil doesn't understand and doesn't want to be a part of, he'd rather not get involved in any of it. Add to that are the slaves—easier to just not see that stuff.

Walking down the boarding ramp, Wil takes a last look at everyone. "Okay, remember: get only what we absolutely need, then get back here. Bennie and Gabe, the Tech sector is out the main gates, to the right. Gabe, keep an active comm link with the rest of us, and if you hear me say 'run', stop what you're doing and get back to the *Ghost* as fast as you can."

The tall bot and the tiny hacker nod, and then head off on their errand. Wil turns to Zephyr and Maxim.

"Okay you two, let's get this done."

Every spaceport and shopping district in the galaxy has a night market. Some are no more than two shabby stalls, some are square blocks or kilometers wide. Despite their size, they're often still not obvious to those not looking—hidden behind dull and vague storefronts, or underground in abandoned caverns. Knowing how to spot and enter a night market is a skill unto itself.

Right now, Wil walks towards what looks like a stall selling fabric. Grabbing a bolt of dark blue fabric, he calls to the shopkeep, "Does this come in a darker shade?"

The shopkeep—an aging Partherian—woman, looks at Wil, then

at the two ex-Peacekeepers, then reaches under the cash register. A section of wall behind her opens; bolts of fabric draped over the seams make it impossible to see the door until it's open. Wil hands her the bolt of fabric and walks in. Zephyr and Maxim follow.

On the display screen mounted in the corner of the shop, the screen cuts to a GNO broadcast. "If you're just joining us, things out on the frontier are getting heated. The warring Harrith factions have again let their conflict spill outside their system, as the rebels harassing the legitimate government of Harrith Prime have once again attacked the Zengar. This time, a deep-space station on the outer edge of the Zengar system has been bombed. This is another violation of the sovereign borders of the Zengar, and risks GC intervention. Already, the GC has deployed four Peacekeeper carriers to the system, with more promised should the need arise. GNO will keep you up to date on this developing situation. This is Mon-el Furash, with GNO."

THE NIGHT MARKET

Every night market is different: some are close to respectable looking; others are dark dungeons you'd rather never visit. This one is somewhere in the middle—likely due to it being the largest on the planet, and nearest to the most populous city and spaceport. Just when Wil is talking himself into being semi-okay with the place, he sees a stall advertising young women of a dozen different species. Of course, none are actually in the booth—that'd be too risky. These slaver booths simply promote the goods, take payment, and set up the rendezvous arrangements. Fuming, Wil increases his pace until he is past the stall, Zephyr and Maxim trailing behind him.

This market is entirely underground. The entrance at the fabric seller's booth had led down a short ramp to what must have been an abandoned mass-transit system, or at least part of one. The bulk of the market was set up in what must have once been a large shopping atrium for passengers. Some of the lesser stalls are set up nearer the transit tracks and tunnels.

"You know, I've never been to a night market I wasn't raiding," Zephyr says, as they pass a stall selling personal weaponry that's outlawed everywhere the Peacekeepers have a say. "It's remarkable how they can be so established."

Wil looks back at her. "Yeah, you might be surprised how many of these markets have someone in Peacekeeper command—or for that matter, the GC directly—on speed dial on their wrist comms. This way." He heads down an artificial alleyway created by the back walls of several more permanent stalls. They turn another corner, around a stall that's nearly double the size of every other one they've seen, and find themselves in what is signposted as 'Armament Alley.' Wil looks up at the sign.

"Cute."

Gabe and Bennie have a far easier task than the others. The tech sector is, for one thing, completely legal. For another, Gabe's shopping list isn't that long. They see a storefront advertising exotic parts, and—seeing as an Ankarran Raptor is definitely on the exotic side—they decide their odds are better here.

"Welcome, my friends!" says the shopkeeper, who is also clearly a Brailack.

"Oh, dren," mutters Bennie. Gabe looks down at his companion, then back to the shopkeeper.

"What can I help you with today?"

Since Bennie isn't speaking up, Gabe decides to. "We are seeking three type-G power regulators and two type-109B thermocouples. Also, if you have them, we are in need of fifteen plasma regulators, type 2."

The shopkeeper beams. "Well, well! That's quite the shopping list. You've come to the right place—not many shops here have parts for Ankarran ships. A raptor, I think. Yes?" He looks between the robot and the Brailack standing with it, smiling.

"You are..." Gabe begins, before Bennie cuts Gabe off, raising a hand to silence the bot.

"Yeah, our ship is Ankarran. You have the parts we need? So that you know, price is paramount. We don't need shiny and new. Let's see your refurb stock."

"Good sir!" the shopkeep protests, "we only sell top of the..."

Bennie raises his hands. "Okay, we're leaving. I'm sure there's another shop that has what we need." As he turns to leave, dragging a confused Gabe with him, the small shopkeep scurries after them, running around to block their exit.

"Okay, Okay, you clearly know what you're doing. Come on, I'll show you my stock. Let's talk price." The three head to the back of the shop.

An immensely confusing (for Gabe) hour later, he and Bennie are leaving the shop carrying four overstuffed boxes. Bennie is beaming and crowing about how great a negotiator he is, and how lucky they are that he was able to get the shopkeep to throw in a brand-new protein sequencer with their purchase. "You know how much better this one will work versus the one on the *Ghost*? I'll finally be able to eat something that doesn't taste like a fart!" Bennie exclaims.

Gabe looks down at Bennie, optic sensors whirring. "I am sure the others will be very pleased."

His days pass quickly. Wil spends all of it on the bridge—all of it, that is, that isn't taken up with grabbing something to eat in the kitchen or taking care of other needs in the small head, which he's found it located behind the bridge, next to the airlock antechamber.

By the time the *Reaper* enters orbit over Fury, Wil has a basic grasp of how to pilot an Ankarran Raptor (which is what he's discovered the *Reaper* is), though landing on a planet might still be a bit out of his skill set still.

"Computer, are you able to assist me in landing the ship?"

"Affirmative," comes the emotionless response.

Wil wonders if the computer realizes how close it is to crashing into a planet and exploding. "Good. Please guide me the through the process, take over if I give the command. Is that understood?"

"Affirmative. Incoming comms from Fury Space Control."

"Put them through, audio only." Wil would prefer no one to know he's the only one on the ship.

"This is Fury Space Control," barks a voice. "Please state your business."

Though nervous, Wil manages to negotiate a landing pad at a

low-rent spaceport. He could afford better. The ship's account is fairly healthy, but he doesn't know how long it'll be until he can make more money, or how much it'll take to doctor up some records.

The landing goes smoothly—or at least as smoothly as Wil could hope for, given that he's never landed a spaceship on an alien planet before, despite the few bumps and hiccups along the way and a near collision with a bulk freighter. That had resulted in a lot of screaming, both from the freighter and from Space Control.

The spaceport isn't all that impressive, even to Wil, who's never been on an alien world before. It's overcrowded, smoggy, and congested, just like Los Angeles. Granted, the occupants are all alien races: tall and short, blue, green, purple and red, tentacled, multi-limbed, slug-like, and even gelatinous, but otherwise not really that different. *God, am I already getting used to this?* Wil wonders.

"Computer, secure the ship," he says, as he walks down the boarding ramp. "No one allowed on or near until I return. If anyone tries, issue one warning, then fire."

"Acknowledged." The inner doors to the cargo area close behind him.

Wil wanders the spaceport for a few hours, before catching on to how it's set up. There is the obvious surface layout: clothiers, food stalls, technology shops, all in little groupings. But then he starts to see the underlying organization. Thankfully, being a human among beings who either don't know what a human is, or do and find it interesting, helps them open up when he asks questions. Another hour of wandering about, and he's knocking on a door to a storefront that looks like it hasn't been occupied in years.

The door opens, and small face pokes out. "What do you want?"

"Your help," Wil says. He's not sure this is a good idea, but from what he's been able to piece together, the being behind this door is his best bet for actually surviving the next few weeks.

The door opens, and Wil enters, before it slams shut behind him. As his eyes adjust, he sees that his potential savior is a roughly four-foot-tall green alien, with a big head. The being walks ahead of him, through an anteroom which has a shimmering privacy field over the doorway. Beyond is a workshop that puts NASA to shame. There are monitors everywhere, and computer consoles of various sizes and shapes.

The small being turns. "So, what do you want?" It points to a stool on the opposite side of a work bench. Wil sits down and begins to outline his problem.

"Easy," the alien says. "You got money? This won't be cheap. Also, we'll have to do the last of the work on your ship."

Wil spends another three hours sitting in what the small being— Ben-Ari, he said his name is—calls his 'customer lounge.' There's not much to do in this lounge other than sit and watch some alien news channel, which seems to be the only thing—other than porn—that Ben-Ari streams into his little hacker's den.

Finally, the alien says, "I'm done, here." He tosses a bracelet-like thing to Wil, who catches it easily. "That's a wrist comm. I'm sure you saw them on your old crew. When we get to your ship, I'll tie the wrist comm to your ship's computer systems, after I've changed its name and registration data."

The walk back to the spaceport is certainly shorter than Wil's original journey. Less than an hour after leaving Ben-Ari's shop, they're in the *Reaper*'s computer access area, located in the engineering space. Ben-Ari is crawling around inside the computer core, while Wil sits at a workbench, exploring the features of his new wrist comm.

"Hey! Human," Ben-Ari calls, as he crawls back out of the access space, tablet in hand. "What do you want to call your new ship?"

Wil looks around the engineering space, thinking of Jax and Rolo, of Ulgo and Lanksham, the two other crew members he never got to know, all of whom died in the Hulgian space station. *Ghosts* who Wil will never forget. Beings who could have killed him when they found him or left him to die in his pod, but who instead showed him a kindness not common in the galaxy. *Ghosts*.

"She's the *Ghost*. That's her name. *Ghost*."

Ben-Ari nods, "The *Ghost*, good name." He taps on this tablet a few times. "Done."

CHAPTER 13

REPAIRS

As Wil and his team approach the *Ghost*, they see that Gabe and Bennie have returned, and are already hard at work. Gabe is standing on a work-lift, reaching deep inside the port engine pod. Bennie is also on the lift, a data terminal in hand, providing the engineering bot with diagnostic information. Seeing the others approach, Bennie sets the terminal down. "How'd it go?"

Before Wil can answer, Maxim does. "It went well! I can't wait for someone to challenge us!" Behind the three rumbles a large cargo bot, with a trailer attached. Bennie whistles.

Maxim directs the bot under the ship, to where the missile bay is located behind the boarding ramp. Zephyr heads up the ramp and into the ship.

Wil walks over to the maintenance lift, looking up at Bennie and Gabe's legs. "How'd it go with you two? I assume you got the parts you need, since Gabe is waist deep in an engine pod?"

One of Gabe's smaller secondary hands makes a thumbs-up gesture. Bennie nods vigorously, "We sure did. Got everything on Gabe's list, and I got the shopkeep to throw in a new protein sequencer, free of charge."

Wil smiles, patting Bennies leg. "Good work! That sequencer is older than the ship, I think. How long before we can take off?"

Bennie looks at his terminal. "We've already replaced the parts in the starboard engine, and Gabe is almost done here. Everything else can be done on the way... I'd say another tock at the most. Unless Maxim needs more than that to load up the weapons."

"A tock should be fine. Maxim! We leave in a tock. Make sure everything is loaded!" There's a grunt, and something mumbled from the back end of the ship, which Wil assumes is a yes. He pats Bennie on the leg again, and heads up into the ship.

Zephyr is waiting on the bridge when he walks in. "Wil," she says. "I wanted to say thank you. I know this isn't your fight. I still don't even know why you rescued Maxim and me from the Partherians, but you're risking your life and your ship. I can't thank you enough. I know even if we're successful, it won't change much for Maxim and I. We won't be able to go back to being Peacekeepers, and honestly, I don't think I'd want to, knowing what I know now."

She doesn't break eye contact with him, as she adds, "This could change the fabric of the sector."

Wil falls into his chair with a sigh. "No thanks needed—and not because I'd be doing this regardless, or that I'm just that noble. Honestly, if I hadn't met you and Max, this wouldn't be happening, and I'd probably be okay with that. But here we are, and it has to be done. Plus, with the exception of almost dying, it's been pretty fun, so far."

He looks at Zephyr, thinking.

"I never told you, back then when I rescued you and Maxim—I never said why I rescued you, did I?" He looks down at his hands. "I've owned the *Ghost* for about three cycles, now. Well, I guess 'owned' isn't the right word, exactly. I'm the only survivor of its previous crew." He raises a hand, as he can see her forming a question. "That's a story for another time. The thing that's important is this: about a cycle ago, the loneliness finally got to me. I had been alone on the *Ghost* all this time, doing whatever jobs I could get to keep the engines running and the ships account's flush. Only so many jobs a single person, even one as awesome as me, can do, though."

He sighs and looks up at the ceiling.

"I started looking for... I don't know, misfits. People like me—alone, broken, nowhere to go. I didn't know what I was looking for, I just knew somewhere deep down that I couldn't keep going alone, not anymore. Too many close calls, too many celebrations alone in the lounge. So when Xarrix mentioned the two Peacekeepers, abandoned by their own organization, and about to live out their days in a Partherian work camp, I figured I'd take a look."

Wil spreads his hands wide. "And here we are."

Zephyr is speechless. She's wondered about this, ever since she first met Wil, all those weeks ago. She remembers him not answering that first day. She remembers him never bringing it up again. She's known it had to come up eventually, but figured it was his story to tell. But in all the versions of this conversation she'd run through in her head, none matched what he'd just told her.

She sits there a moment more, before saying anything. "I see. Well for what it's worth—and I know I speak for Maxim as well—we're happy here. We've only known you, and Bennie, for that matter, a short time—Gabe even shorter—and we're at least friends." She pauses. "But it feels more than that. Peacekeepers aren't known for our social entanglements... but this is the closest I've felt to family, in a long time."

Wil nods. "Yeah, Bennie certainly wasn't in the plan. Gabe certainly wasn't, either. But I can't say I'm not glad they're here."

They both sit quietly for a few minutes, each deep in thought over what the other has said, each enjoying the silence and company.

Then the moment is ruined by Bennie entering the bridge. "Come on krebnakcs, we're all set. So let's get the hell out of here!"

LIKE NEW

The *Ghost* is four hours from Harrith Prime, everyone but Gabe is on the bridge. Bennie is at his station—originally an auxiliary station, but now a hackers' hideaway, covered in a cobweb of data cables and additional displays epoxied to the hull. Zephyr is at her own station, assuming the role of second-in-command, and Maxim is at the tactical station. The large ex-Peacekeeper is beaming, which is disconcerting, to say the least.

Most of the stations on the bridge of the *Ghost* look similar to one other—or they had before Bennie came aboard. Tactical is the exception, with its additional displays and manual weapon control surfaces —'the works', as Maxim calls it.

"Now, this is what I've been wanting!" he exclaims, caressing his terminal. "So. Many. Weapons. The engine mounted disruptors are both at one hundred percent. The Forward section disrupter turret, also one hundred percent! The targeting computer firmware is up to date; I could target Bennie drifting out there from nearly a half million kilometers away, and hit him with a single shot!"

"Hey!" comes the screech from Bennie's station. "Why would you say that?!"

Wil nods, smiling. It's nice to see Maxim happy about something, but also nice to know the *Ghost* is in fighting shape; something she's slipped further and further away from since Wil took over. "Missiles?" he asks.

Maxim taps a few sections of his panel. "Both missile magazines are full. I was able to score a few multi-model ones: full yield, medium, or 'overload shields.' Plus..." he pauses, and his grin turns a bit evil. "I got six XPX-1900s."

Zephyr lets out a low whistle. "I don't remember getting those."

"Me either," Wil chimes in. "Also, what are they?"

Maxim looks at Zephyr, then back at Wil. "Ship busters."

"The fuck?!" Wil exclaims, leaning out of his chair. "How did you manage to score those without Zephyr or I seeing—or bankrupting us, *or* alerting the Peacekeepers or even just the local police?"

The large Palorian grins. "After we made our purchases, and you and Zephyr were on your way out. I asked the shopkeep for a favor. I thought I'd noticed them in the back of the shop in a corner. Selling that type of ordinance is, if it's possible, extra illegal. He'd had them a few years and never found anyone to take them, at least for a price he was willing to take the risk for."

"Okay. But since we hardly had any credits left, there's no way you could've pay that price, whatever it was," Wil says.

"Right, but I dropped some hints that we'd likely be quite popular, and/or wealthy, if this mission goes well. Since he'd been sitting on them so long... and given that even being caught with them, selling them or not, would land him a life sentence on a Peacekeeper labor moon... he just gave them to me."

Bennie, who's been listening intently, chimes in. "Maybe I have some competition for this crew's chief negotiator?"

Wil looks at the hacker. "Who says that role is filled by you, pipsqueak?"

Bennie affects a stricken look and seems about to protest when he scrunches his face up. "What's a pip squeak?"

In unison, Zephyr and Maxim both say: "A human thing."

Just then, Gabe's voice comes over the speakers. "Captain, please come to engineering."

Wil hits a button on his chair. "On my way. Zephyr, keep us moving in the right direction—and don't let Bennie touch my console."

The *Ghost* is not a large ship; the forward section is only made up of two decks, the bridge, the staging area-cum-armory and airlocks, with a maintenance area below. The main corridor—or 'neck', as Wil refers to it—is nearly as long as the primary section of the ship: one deck, plus maintenance spaces above and below. It gets a bit taller as you move into the main body of the ship, where the crew space and lounge is, with engineering directly beyond. Wil walks through it all, remembering the first time he was in the lounge.

The hatch to engineering is closed when he approaches. He touches the control pad beside it, and a light turns green and the doors open.

"Gabe, what's up? Oh. My. God." The entire engineering space is spotless. The main engine is thrumming peacefully—the random hiccup that had plagued the drive apparently gone. The stains on the bulkhead that Wil was always afraid to ask about are also gone. The maintenance area and workbench: spotless. The heat that normally permeated the place: also gone.

"Hello, Captain. I wanted to give you a status update on the engineering space. As you can see, I've fixed the imbalance in the main FTL drive. I've also cleaned, and replaced all the burnt-out thermocouples, which has addressed the increased heat in this compartment. Several other subsystems have been repaired, or, in extreme cases, replaced."

Wil is spinning around, taking it all in. "You're a miracle-worker. I wonder if there's another smaller you in that shoulder thingy."

Gabe looks at the mysterious attachment. "I highly doubt there is a smaller copy of myself in this device."

Wil shakes his head. "Whatever it is, good work, Gabe. It's awesome that you're with us—"

Before he can say anything more, Zephyr interrupts over the ship's intercom, "Wil, you better get up here. There's something you need to see."

Wil turns and leaves without another word.

As the hatch to engineering closes, Gabe bows his head slightly. "Thank you, Captain."

THE PAST

After Ben-Ari finishes his work on the ship, Wil spends another week on Fury. The small hacker has assured him that the identity change would propagate to the old log files of the Fury Space Control, so that the *Reaper* isn't logged as landing while the *Ghost* is logged as leaving. Wil spends much of his time on the ship, running through its training mode, which he discovers isn't limited to the flight controls. While engineering isn't his strong suit, he's been able to get the ship to at least train him on how to identify the more serious problems—even if he doesn't possess the skill to fix them. He uses a little more of his dwindling cash to hire an engineer to come aboard and give the engineering space a once over, addressing any major issues. Luckily, the previous engineering team had done a pretty good job of keeping the engines shipshape.

Once he's sure the ship is in as good a condition as possible, he ventures back into the shopping district and beyond. Ben-Ari has given him a rudimentary map, marked with places to avoid and places where he might find work—sorted by the kind of work he might be okay with, from mercenary work to smuggling to basic freight hauling. Wil isn't sure which he's comfortable with, but is pretty sure that the former is out; if nothing else, he's not sure how good he'd be at that type of work without a crew.

Hiring a crew is also out. Wil doesn't know the first thing about leading others, nor does he know who he could trust, or what races work best with others. Plus, based on what's left in the ship's accounts, he's pretty sure the crew he could afford would kill him and sell the *Ghost* at the first opportunity.

He wanders into a bar that Ben-Ari flagged as having potential for work of the non-mercenary type. Sitting at the bar, he orders a drink—grum, which has become his new favorite beverage, if for no other reason than it's ubiquitousness, and has reliable side effects. He knows he can get a buzz, and even shit-faced, but it works so like beer that he can manage it. Almost everything else on the menu is liquors from around the sector he has no idea about. One sip could lay him out, which wouldn't be good.

Unfortunately, Ben-Ari's map and notes aren't tremendously helpful, or at least informative. The notation on this bar is simply the word 'Xarrix.' *Whatever or whomever that is,* Wil thinks. He flags down the barkeep, and leans forward. "Does 'Xarrix' mean anything to you? I'm looking for it, or him or her, or whatever."

The barkeep looks at him blankly, then glances over Wil's shoulder to the back of the bar, where several booths sit. All have a privacy screen activated, protecting their occupants from being seen or overheard. The barkeep points to the middle booth. Wil nods and takes a big gulp of grum, steeling his nerves, then gets up and makes his way to the back booths.

As he approaches, two giant aliens move in from the tables nearby. Wil has no idea what race they are. He's never seen either before—but that's not saying much, really.

"What do you want?" one asks.

Wil looks up. This particular alien is nearly eight feet tall, and is apparently made entirely of muscle.

"I'm looking for Xarrix." The two just stare at him. "I was, uh told that, well, maybe he'd have work for me?" Wil is starting to rethink this whole idea, when the silent one lifts its wrist comm and whispers into it. There's a reply, and the alien whispers some more, before he looks at his colleague and nods. They part and the talkative one points to the booth.

Stepping through the privacy field and into the booth, Wil sees that Xarrix is indeed a who, though of a race Wil can't identify either--something vaguely reptilian.

"So you need work, huh?" The alien says, without preamble. "Tell me about your ship."

Wil does his best to describe the *Ghost*, without revealing it's a warship. He's hoping this doesn't come up. Instead, he emphasizes his desire to haul cargo and maybe, if needed, to smuggle it. Ten minutes later, he leaves the booth with his first paying gig as the owner of a spaceship. *Not bad for a human,* he thinks to himself, walking out into the street beyond.

CHAPTER 14

HITTING THE FAN

"Coming to you from the Peacekeeper Carrier Pax Magellanic, I'm Mon-el Furash with GNO. The Peacekeepers have welcomed us— and you—aboard one of their most impressive carriers on the front lines of this conflict on the frontier. Just the other day, the Harrith rebels bombed a trade depot which, at the time of the attack, had two Quilant Trade Federation freighters docked within it. Both were destroyed, and their crews killed. The Harrith Navy was able to track down one of the rebel vessels and destroy it, but the other two were able to escape. Understandably, the Quilant are demanding restitution and revenge, and their fleet is reported to be en route to the Harrith system. Stay tuned for updates as events unfold. Back to you, Xyrzix and Megan."

"Would you look at that? That's a lot of firepower," Bennie says, as the primary display resolves into four Peacekeeper carriers holding position in space, surrounded by a dozen or so smaller Peacekeeper vessels. Twenty or thirty Zengar ships, considerably smaller than the Peacekeeper vessels, flit around the four large warships. Opposite them, still within the boundaries of the Harrith system, is a small fleet of Harrith Defense Force ships; only one is the size of a Peacekeeper ship, with the rest much smaller.

"Should we go around?" Maxim asks.

Zephyr looks up from her station. "Even at FTL; it'd take too long. With the Quilant on their way, the Harrith will have no choice but to acquiesce and allow the Peacekeepers into the system to help squash the rebellion. If they don't, they face being forcibly invaded, and drawn into a war they can't hope to win. If they give in, the GC has a strong foothold and a reason to push for them to join, and if they resist, the GC will have a strong foothold, and the firepower to force them to join. Sucks to be the rebels right now—no matter what happens, they're likely about to be wiped out, by the very people who've been supplying them."

Bennie looks up from his station. "Moot point."

No sooner has the last word left his mouth than a few dozen warships drop out of FTL, directly between the Peacekeeper forces and their allies and the Harrith Navy, and immediately opening fire in every direction at every ship, Peacekeeper and Harrith Navy alike. Ships start exploding on both sides, taken completely by surprise.

"The Rebels! Damnit!" Wil exclaims, grabbing the controls, bringing the *Ghost* around in a wide arc, off its original course. "Computer, combat alert!" A torpedo whizzes by the ship, exploding just aft, rocking the ship heavily.

Chaos erupts on both sides, as ships accelerate towards the battle, weapons blazing. Two of the Peacekeeper carriers begin launching fighters, while the smaller Zengar ships spread out, forming wolf-packs and chasing the rebel ships. Wil knows that the Zengar do not have a massive navy, since the GC technically protects them with Peacekeepers, but all GC members are allowed to keep a small 'home fleet'. The Zengar, apparently wanting blood after the trade station explosion, seem to have sent their entire home fleet here.

"You got it, combat alert!" the chipper computer replies. "All tactical systems online, shields at full power."

Zephyr is furiously working her console, tagging as many ships as she can. "Looks like the rebels don't realize who's been supplying them. Or just don't care—they're attacking everyone: Peacekeeper, Zengar, and Harrith."

Wil is swinging the ship below a flaming Peacekeeper ship—a Corvette, from the looks of the remains. "Karma. Is. A. Bitch!" he yells. The ship takes a hit, and sparks erupt from overhead. "Max! Weapons free! Focus on the rebels—but Peacekeepers and Harrith are free game too, until we can get clear and find someone to give our information to. Someone shoots at us, shoot right back at 'em!"

Outside the *Ghost*, a flaming Peacekeeper Carrier explodes as it takes two dozen missiles to its port side. Six Harrith rebel ships break formation around the burning carrier. Another wave of ships follows close behind, unleashing more missiles into the flaming side of the massive ship. Escape pods are ejecting from all over the carrier, even while its guns are still firing—some of the crew clearly deciding to go down with the ship, or being told to. Three of the rebel ships explode at that moment; another takes a hit and careens past the dying carrier, right into a Harrith Navy cruiser. Fighters are flitting around taking whatever shots they can, letting their missiles fly in all directions.

The *Ghost* tilts on its wing and flies between two of the larger Harrith Navy ships, shields flaring, disruptors blasting out at the smaller craft in its path. A rebel frigate is directly ahead, and before he can think to give the order, Wil hears the telltale rattle that precedes missiles launching from the lower section of the ship. Suddenly, four missiles break out from under *Ghost*, flying straight for the rebel ship. It tries to out maneuver the fast-moving projectiles, but fails, taking all four on its side. Seconds later, the entire ship cracks in half, as secondary explosions riddle the vessel. The *Ghost* flies right through the gap in the two flaming halves.

Wil lets out a whoop. "Great shooting!"

Zephyr calls out targets, as Maxim continues to work the tactical console. "This is fun!" the big Palorian is shouting, destroying smaller rebel craft with well-placed disruptor bolts. The turret mounted on the upper section of the bridge module is letting loose blasts in all directions.

From the screen in the corner, the GNO feed is still narrating events to the whole galaxy: "... if you're just joining us, things here outside the Harrith system have taken a turn for the—well, 'worse' is putting it mildly. Tempers were already reaching boiling point when a small vessel appeared out of FTL, attempting to enter the Harrith system. It's unclear if these two events are connected, but shortly after this vessel appeared, so did the Harrith rebels. The rebels were only on the scene a fraction of a tock before opening fire on the Peacekeepers, the Harrith Navy, and the Zengar. The entire area has erupted into chaos, with ships firing at each other, seemingly at random." The newscaster pauses, listening to her co-anchors back in the studio. "Yes, Xyrzix, it's been terrifying, but so far the Pax Magellanic has remained safely out of the fight. I'll keep you posted as things develop. For now, back to you and Megan."

GABE

Having decided that standing on the bridge offers very little value, Gabe has spent much of his time in engineering, figuring that this will be a better use of not just his time but capabilities. The days spent in FTL en route to the Harrith system have afforded Gabe time to get to know the crew, as well as the systems of the *Ghost*. He has to admit, the stories about the Ankarran shipwrights are true: the *Ghost* is an impressive vessel for its size.

He had been busying himself cleaning a spare thermocouple when the ship lurches to one side, the computer announcing, "Combat alert! Secure all sections, all personnel report to battle stations!"

Silently, Gabe sends a wireless connection request to the main computer: *Computer, report please.*

Over the wireless connection, the ship replies: "The Captain has activated the ship's combat systems. Several ships have begun firing, causing all ships in the vicinity to return fire. We are in the cross-fire."

Calmly, Gabe puts the thermocouple and his cleaning supplies away, activating the magnetic components of his feet to keep standing as the ship shakes and rattles from the impacts, lurching in an attempt to avoid enemy fire.

A flashing alert draws his attention: one of the starboard plasma conduits has begun leaking, interfering with other systems nearby. Gabe picks up a portable toolkit, his smaller manipulators holding it against his torso, and enters the starboard service corridor. Similar corridors run from each side of the engineering space the entire length of the ship's wing, ending in a crawlspace in the actual engine pod.

The starboard corridor is already toxic to most oxygen-breathing species by the time Gabe enters it. Plasma from the ruptured conduit is flowing into the area, turning into a toxic gas as it interacts with the ships breathable atmosphere.

Gabe hurries up the corridor to where the breach is indicated, the ship still shaking all around him. Withdrawing a patch kit from his toolkit, he moves aside wiring and other equipment from around the rupture; many wires have already corroded in the gas. As he places the patch over the breach, it magnetically seals itself against the conduit; with the touch of a button on the control pad built into the patch itself, the outer edges of the patch begin to melt, fusing to the conduit. When the indicator on the patch control panel turns green, Gabe returns his attention to the other components nearby, stripping away the corroded insulation and, in some cases, cutting wires and patching new pieces in.

Gabe is returning to engineering when another alert lights on up on the master ship's system display. He immediately hurries out through the main crew space. The airlock leading into the cargo area has snapped closed—there's an enormous breach in the hull, air is whistling out of it. Cycling through the airlock, Gabe grabs a large piece of metal from its resting place against the bulkhead, and lurches towards to the breach. The ships maneuvers aren't helping; despite being able to magnetize his feet, the grav-plating is having a hard time compensating, and the patch in his hands shifts awkwardly.

But he soon has the patch secured, the ship's computer confirming no more leaks. Gabe has made it back to the main crew space when the ship rattles worse than it ever has before, and the sound of wrenching metal fills his sensors. He runs to the engineering area, and, glancing at the master display, rushes into the port service corridor.

"Captain," he says into his comms unit, "our port engine pod has taken several hits. FTL will be impossible if it takes any more abuse." Something catches his attention, perhaps his report to the Captain was optimistic—FTL may be already a non-option.

WORSE, BEFORE IT GETS BETTER

Each time the *Ghost* attempts to make a break deeper into the Harrith system, a rebel, Peacekeeper or Harrith Navy ship intercepts them.

"Captain, our port engine pod has taken several hits," Gabe reports from the engineering space. "FTL will be impossible if it takes any more abuse."

"Doing what I can, Gabe. You do the same!" Swinging the *Ghost* in a tight arc, Wil barely avoids a Zengar cruiser that's flying out of control, flames, and debris falling from it as it goes. "Hold on!" He spins the ship on its axis to avoid what looks like a piece of an FTL engine.

The battle has been raging for close to an hour. One Peacekeeper Carrier is nothing but a wreck; another is limping to the outer edge of the engagement. The Zengar, out for blood, aren't letting the rebels have even a second's rest. The Quilant, who have also arrived, have mainly been engaging the Harrith, only occasionally firing on the rebels if one gets close. Meanwhile, the *Ghost*, as an actual third party, is doing its best not to get destroyed by all sides, who seem to think the *Ghost* is whomever they're angry at.

"We've got to get clear! We're taking too many hits!" Zephyr shouts from her station. "The port Disruptor is on the verge of over-heating, and we're running low on missiles."

Maxim looks over from his station. "We still have the XPX-1900s!"

Wil nods. "We might end up needing them if things keep up like this!" The ship shakes and rocks, and the primary display waivers and crackles with static before returning to normal. A panel to Wil's left explodes, showering him with sparks. Two rebel light-attack craft are swooping around on an attack run. Maxim takes one out using the starboard disruptor, but the other rains weapons-fire across the back of the ship and the neck connecting the forward section.

"Captain, there's a hull breach in the cargo area!" Gabe's voice filters through the alarms blaring on the bridge.

Wil steals a glance at a master system display off to the side of his console—the cargo hold is flashing red, while the crew lounge is slowly pulsing orange, on the verge of losing pressure too. The hatch between the two spaces must have been compromised.

"Do what you can Gabe! Max, get those, XP's ready."

The big Palorian grins evilly. "XPXs and acknowledged."

Bennie, who's been quiet for some time now, pipes up. "Wil, I have an idea."

Wil glances over. "I'm all ears!" The ship corkscrews around a Harrith Navy cruiser, which is slugging it out with a Quilant carrier.

"I've been scanning all the comms chatter since this whole mess started, and I think I've isolated the primary frequencies each faction is using. If we can boost the power of our transmitter, I might be able to broadcast our data to all of them at the same time."

"Gabe, did you hear that?"

"I did, Captain. I will do what I can down here to provide the power that Bennie requires. I need only a few more centocks to address the hull breach."

Wil looks at Bennie. "Get to work."

"This will likely piss off Xarrix and Lorath, you know?" Zephyr points out. "Whatever it is they had planned for this info is about to be undone."

"Can't be helped. If we survive this, we can work on making it up to them. Or avoiding them."

The *Ghost* spins around another Quilant ship, firing its last two regular missiles at a rebel ship that has just fired on a Peacekeeper cruiser. "Max, that largest rebel ship: put two XPXs in it. With the other two, target that Peacekeeper Carrier there." He points at the fourth Peacekeeper carrier on the main display, which has somehow avoided any substantive damage. "That one. They clearly know something—they're staying just out of the main engagement zone."

Maxim nods, working his console. Deep inside the weapon's magazine in the main body of the ship, four of the six XPX-1900 missiles are moving into the forward launchers: two in each chamber, two in the ready loader for each chamber. There are still dozens of ships in the fight, slugging it out, firing whatever they have left at each other. The Zengar, by far the smallest force in this melee, are down to only a few ships, mostly hovering near the lone Peacekeeper Carrier that's entirely undamaged. Another Peacekeeper Carrier is limping away, while yet another burns, and a final one is nothing more than several large chunks of debris.

Two of the ship-buster missiles streak away from the *Ghost* toward the now-doomed rebel ship. Moments later, two massive explosions rip the vessel apart.

The remaining rebels, having probably caused as much confusion as they feel they can, have slowly withdrawn, fighting to extricate themselves in order to make a getaway. The *Ghost* is trailing smoke and drive plasma from its port FTL engine pod, and its port disruptor is offline.

Bennie hoots. "Got it. I'm ready!"

"Gabe, you ready?"

"Yes, Captain."

Wil looks over to Bennie just long enough to nod, "Do it!"

"Once again, I'm Mon-el Furash with GNO, aboard the Peacekeeper Carrier Pax Magellanic, where following the arrival of the Quilant, who have immediately engaged the Harrith Navy and the rebels alike, a small Ankarran Raptor called the *Ghost* has really changed the tenor of this battle." The anchor pauses. "Hectic is putting it mildly, Megan. It's likely that thousands have already died, and more are dying as we speak. It's madness. I don't know if the GC is on board with this, or what the results will be here, but I'll keep reporting to the end."

"Transmitting now!" Bennie announces, hitting a button on his console. His words are largely drowned out by the sound of something exploding against the ship.

THE TRUTH COMES OUT

Zephyr is staring intently at her console. "That Peacekeeper Carrier is now targeting us!" she shouts. "They're accelerating."

Wil nods. "Figured. That must be the ship that has our evildoers on board." He spins the *Ghost* about, and pushes the power controls to the max. The acceleration compensators struggle to do their job, as the *Ghost* flies through the remains of the battle, dodging debris and weapons fire. The Peacekeeper Carrier has turned and is burning after the much smaller ship. The Zengar and Quilant, having received the transmission, have moved off. The Harrith are moving to intercept the *Ghost*, while the rebels are scattering in whatever direction contains the least ships.

"Peacekeeper Carrier is closing the gap," Zephyr reports. "We're almost in their engagement envelope."

Wil looks to Max. "Aft weapons status?"

Maxim looks up from his console, his face not as exuberant as it had been earlier. "Aft missile bay is offline, and our aft disruptor array is non-functional. Shields are at sixty-four percent. I'm afraid our backside isn't well protected."

"They're closing, Wil!" Zephyr announces, looking from her console to Wil.

Wil glances around at his crew. "Anything from, well, anyone? A response to our transmission?"

"The Harrith are on an intercept course, but still a few fractions of a tock out; the Peacekeepers will get to us first," Zephyr reports. "No one has replied to our transmission, though the Peacekeepers are trying to jam all comms now."

The ship rocks and Wil grabs the controls, banking the ship hard to port. More sparks and smoke erupt from a panel near Bennie's station, eliciting a screech from the small hacker.

"Oh shit!" Wil yelps, slamming his controls to the side, spinning the stars on the display and barely avoiding one of the Harrith Navy cruisers. "Sorry, didn't see them there!" He smooths out their flight, as the Harrith ship opens fire on the Peacekeeper Carrier.

"Oh, it's on!" Bennie shouts. "They're engaging the Peacekeeper carrier!"

Zephyr is studying her console. "They don't stand a chance. That ship avoided the fighting, it's fresh. It'll destroy them."

Bennie leaves his station to stand next to Wil. "Better them than us." In response, Wil punches him in the arm, which sends the smaller alien flying across the bridge. "Ouch! That hurt!!"

Wil looks at Maxim. "Let's even the odds." When Maxim raises an eyebrow questioningly, he only nods. "You didn't fire those two chambered ship busters, right?"

The big ex-Peacekeeper doesn't break eye contact with Wil, but reaches down and taps a key on his console. Quietly, he says, "One XPX-1900, away."

The sound of a single missile firing reverberates through the hull. On the screen, it streaks outwards, before banking sharply and turning past the ship.

Wil adjusts the primary display, switching to an aft-facing camera. The big Peacekeeper ship is engaged with a half dozen Harrith ships: two are drifting, one still firing as it also drifts away from the engagement. No one seems to notice the XPX-1900 until it's too late.

The missile strikes the big ship amidships, cracking it in half, and causing hundreds of secondary explosions to ripple through its surface. The Harrith Naval vessels break wide, avoiding the explosions. As they watch, lifeboats begin streaking out of the dying Peacekeeper ship in all directions.

Everyone on the bridge lets out a shout of triumph—quickly interrupted by Gabe. "Captain, the port wing stabilizer has taken extensive damage. Controls will be sluggish. I suggest you keep our speed at no more than three quarters max. We are going to need a space dock to affect repairs."

"Keep an eye on it, Gabe." Wil adjusts their speed, sliding the main sub-light thruster controls down a few notches, dropping their speed. He alters their course for the main Harrith home world. Grimly, he asks, "Gabe, will we make it to Harrith Prime?"

"If we can avoid further damage to our control systems... perhaps," the bot replies. "It is possible I can go out on the hull and effect a temporary repair to the port stabilizer assembly. It will not be a permanent fix, I am afraid."

"Incoming comms from the Harrith Navy, the lead ship," Zephyr announces.

"On screen," Wil orders.

The primary display, still wobbling and static-laden at times, switches from the stars to a smoky command center filled with harried and bloodied Harrith. A female officer is front and center on the screen.

"Thank you," she says. "I don't know who you are, or what you are even. But the people of Harrith owe you a debt of gratitude. I am Commander Shre' ta'n of the Harrith Navy." She bows, deeply.

"You're welcome. I'm Wil Calder, and this is my crew..." Before Wil can finish, the *Ghost* shakes and lurches to the side, Zephyr shouting a warning. On the screen, filling with static, the Harrith ship is lurching as well.

Three new Peacekeeper Carriers have dropped out of FTL,

nearly on top of the remaining Harrith Navy and the *Ghost*, unleashing every weapon they have on their prey.

Smoke is filling the bridge. Maxim, Zephyr, and Bennie are all shouting. On the screen, Commander Shre' ta'n is shouting orders at her bridge crew. She turns back to the camera, and Wil. "Get to Harrith Prime!" she shouts. Then the screen fills with static, and returns to the blank of the star field.

"Xyrzix and Megan, things have gone from really bad to terrible here outside the Harrith system! The Pax Magellanic is no more, having taken a direct hit of some type, which snapped the mighty ship in half! Moments before the ship exploded, the Ankarran Raptor, the *Ghost*, transmitted a data packet, which, well, if true, is immensely damning to the Peacekeepers and the GC." Smoke is everywhere in the background, as the newscaster raises her voice. "I'm currently aboard an escape pod with my camera-bot and a few of the Pax Magellanic's crew. We barely escaped alive, as shortly after the *Ghost* transmitted its data the ship exploded." The pod shakes and Mon-El lets out a brief scream. One of the Peacekeepers says something the camera doesn't pick up. "Oh, good," the newscaster says, turns back to the camera. "I've been informed that a Quilant cruiser has recovered our pod. I say again, the data transmitted by the *Ghost* is incredibly damning to the Peacekeepers and likely to many others within the GC. I'm Mon-el Furash with GNO, live from an escape pod. Back to you in the studio."

PART FIVE

CHAPTER 15

RUN!

"Get to Harrith Prime!" is the last thing Wil hears, before a loud screeching comes from Bennie's station. That entire section of the bridge is smoking, sparks and flame are everywhere.

"Bennie!" Wil is already out of his seat and grabbing the unconscious hacker, dragging him clear of the destroyed station. The ship lurches again, and the sound of metal tearing fills the bridge.

Zephyr rushes over and pushes Wil away. "Fly!" She yells at him, over the noise.

Wil lurches up and staggers back to his station. "Gabe, report!" He's fighting the controls now, trying to avoid fire from the new warships.

The overhead speakers crackle and hiss, before Gabe's voice comes through. "Significant damage to the central corridor. I am afraid it looks like the bridge is cut off from the rest of the vessel. In addition, the port engine pod has suffered extensive damage. It is now only ten percent functional. FTL is impossible; the weapons array is damaged, as is the repulsor system for landing and atmospheric flight. Also, that stabilizer is no longer an issue."

Wil perks up. "It's fixed?"

"It is gone."

"Dren!" Wil is fighting to keep the ship moving in the general direction of Harrith Prime, but the damage has made maneuvering difficult. Even at top speed out running a Peacekeeper Carrier is unlikely—at only three-quarters of their capacity, it's impossible. Normally, it would still be a fair fight, as the much smaller warship is far more agile, and can easily out-maneuver the larger ship. But that advantage is almost entirely gone now. "Is there anything you can do, Gabe?"

Over the speakers, one the few that remain active, the bot replies: "I am afraid not, Captain. I will continue to look for options."

Wil looks over at Zephyr and the prone Bennie. "How's he doing?"

She looks up. "He's not dead, so there's that. He'll need a doctor, or an autodoc, soon. Looks like his arm and leg are broken, and there's a gash on his head. His breathing is strong, so that's good."

Wil turns back to his controls. The Peacekeepers are currently being distracted by the remaining Harrith Navy, but the remains of that force are not much of a match for them. "Maxim, check the main corridor. See if you can get through or seal off the damage. Maybe we can get Bennie to the medbay. Not much more you can do at tactical now, anyway."

The big man gets up. "On it." Wil can hear him calling Gabe on his wrist comm as he hurries out of the bridge.

"Incoming hail," the computer announces.

"From whom?" Wil asks.

"Commander Janus, Senior Peacekeeper Commander, Belrus Sector. His description."

Wil and Zephyr exchange looks. "Put him through."

The screen, still riddled with static, changes from a view of stars to what Wil can only describe as an eel in a Peacekeeper uniform. "Janus, good to see you again!" Wil says. He taps a few controls on his console.

On the screen the Peacekeeper sneers, taking in the wreck that is the bridge of the *Ghost*. "You've looked better, Wil Calder. Why not shut your engines down and surrender. Maybe you don't even have to die—I'm sure we can find a rock to hide you under. After you admit publicly to doctoring that transmission, of course."

Zephyr steps into the camera's range. "Never, Janus. You and every corrupt Peacekeeper will burn for this."

Janus' smile gets wider. "Well, well, I'd wondered what happened to you and Maxim. I had heard that the Partherians lost you, but would never have guessed you'd end up with this human. Taking on a crew finally, Wil? Better for me—all my loose ends in one convenient wrapper. As I said, surrender now—you're going to die anyway, but it doesn't have to be painful or drawn out. I understand asphyxiating from a hull breach is rather unpleasant."

"Megan, Xyrzix, things are getting very exciting and dangerous around here. We're aboard the Quilant cruiser now, but I don't know if we're any safer. Four more Peacekeeper Carriers have arrived, and we've just received what can only be described as a final nail in the Peacekeeper's coffin. The Commander of these four new vessels seems to know the captain of the *Ghost*, who we now know is a being named Wil Calder. The conversation between the two was quite telling, and—whether intentional or not—was broadcast entirely over an open channel." She looks off screen and blanches a bit, but nods. "I've just been informed that the commander of the Quilant forces has been in conference with the Harrith and their rebels, as well as the Zengar. I'm not told what's next, but I suspect that, whatever it is, it'll be big."

Wil opens his mouth to tell Janus exactly what he can do with his ultimatum when Zephyr points to the tactical display near Maxim's station. "Look!"

Before Wil can do anything, he sees the bridge around Janus erupt into chaos and shake slightly.

Wil hits a control on his console, ending the call with Janus and switching to a tactical view. On screen, he sees nearly three dozen ships converging on the Peacekeeper task force. The Quilant, the Harrith rebels, and the Zengar must have had a little pow-wow while the Peacekeepers were chasing the *Ghost*.

The newly formed anti-Peacekeeper fleet is buzzing around the four Carriers, doing a fair bit of damage, but overall losing more than they're winning.

"Wil, those ships aren't going to last long. Those Carriers aren't pulling their punches," Zephyr reports, back at her station.

Maxim re-enters the bridge. "What's going on?"

"Oh you know, the usual. Lots of ships, all fighting each other. Janus is a dick, and he knows you and Zephyr are here. The usual. Where's Bennie?" Wil turns his chair to face Maxim, seeing only now that he's in his Peacekeeper power armor.

"Gabe and I were able to repair the damage to the main corridor... enough to re-pressurize it temporarily and get Bennie to the medbay. The autodoc is working on him. What's our status?"

"We're being chased by four Peacekeeper Carriers, who're being attacked by an alliance of all the parties, who were until recently trying to kill each other. Janus is aboard the lead ship."

Maxim growls and stomps over to the tactical station. Wil turns in his chair, watching him.

"Most of our weapons systems are offline," Maxim says. "But we still have three XPX-1900s."

The ship shakes, as a hit strikes the aft shields—or what is left of them. "The forward missile magazine is damaged," Maxim reports. "But two of the XPX-1900s are in the port launcher, though, one in the tube, one in the chamber."

"Wil, those Carriers aren't slowing," Zephyr interrupts. "The fleet is doing their best, but they're already down to half their starting strength."

Wil brings the ship around hard, metal groaning from the strain as the inertial compensators struggle. "Maxim, fire on the nearest carrier!"

Without a word, Maxim hits the command on his console. Throughout the ship, the sound of the launcher expelling its lethal load reverberates. On the fizzing, damaged main screen, a lone missile streaks out of the *Ghost*, aiming straight at one of the oncoming carriers.

One missile among hundreds being fired by all sides isn't easy to spot, and is even harder to shoot down. The XPX-1900 hits the Peacekeeper carrier head-on, burrowing right through the hull before it explodes, triggering hundreds of secondary explosions all down the length of the massive spaceship. The remaining three carriers try to move away from the stricken vessel, still fighting off the remnants of the quickly-formed fleet.

With a last look, Wil brings the *Ghost* back around on its course to Harrith Prime, just as Gabe walks into the bridge.

"There is not much I can do in engineering at this point. I am sorry, Captain." The big engineering bot looks at Bennie's station. "Where is Bennie?"

Without looking up, Maxim answers, "Still in medbay."

Without another word, the Gabe turns and exits the bridge.

"Incoming!" Maxim shouts. The main display switches to a view aft, showing a wave of incoming missiles. "We can't absorb that many hits," The big man warns.

"We don't have the maneuverability to dodge them!" Wil reports, slamming his hands against his console.

"Look!" Zephyr shouts, drawing their attention back to the static-filled display. Several ships are speeding towards the *Ghost*—or rather, the space directly behind the *Ghost*. They intercept the wave of missiles, each ship being engulfed in flames.

For a moment, the crew of the *Ghost* just watch, dumbstruck.

"All those people," Zephyr says, faintly.

"They're buying us time." Wil grabs his console and flight controls. "Maxim, get that last XPX ready!" The ship banks hard again, groaning with the effort. "Hang in there..." Wil whispers. "We need to shake these carriers enough to get a lead! Maxim, when I say the word, fire the missile between the two nearest ships, then detonate.

Maxim nods. The *Ghost* has swung a full one-hundred-and-eighty degrees and is flying right toward the Peacekeeper force, which their now-allies are still attempting to destroy. The one remaining Disruptor on the starboard engine pod lances out at the oncoming ships.

"Fire!"

The *Ghost* banks just as the deadly missile launches. Shaking with each hit the diminished shields take, consoles all over the ship are bursting into flames, showering everyone in sparks.

"Hang on!" Wil shouts, as the ship shakes violently, still taking hits from all sides. The already-damaged port engine pod sheers off, taking a large portion of the wing with it. The sound of tearing metal fills the ship. Then the main screen goes dark, followed almost immediately by the rest of the bridge.

ALLIES TO THE RESCUE

A second later the lights come back up; the primary display comes back online, still mostly static. The *Ghost* is limping along, diving deeper into the Harrith system, still heading for Harrith Prime. The last available XPX-1900 missile has been fired, damaging the two nearest Peacekeeper Carriers, but not destroying them.

"Wil, they'll be back in weapons range in a few more fractions of a tock," Zephyr reports.

"All tactical systems are offline," Maxim adds from his station.

Wil sighs. "And we're down to about fifty percent thrust on the sub-light engines. I've got the throttle at the stops, but we're just not moving. I'm sorry, guys."

The hatch to the bridge opens, and Gabe re-enters. "Bennie is stable," he reports.

Wil turns to look at the bot. "Not sure if that's better or worse for him." He turns back to face the main display. "Guessing there's nothing else you can do in engineering?"

The big engineering bot shakes his head. "I am afraid not, captain. The damage is quite extensive. I've patched the main reactor as much as I can without risking it going critical. However, it is likely it will still do exactly that, and soon."

"It's fine, Gabe. We wouldn't have made it this far without you. Thanks," Wil says, wearily. "You might as well go keep an eye on Bennie, since the rest of us can't easily get back there right now, I'm guessing?"

"That is correct. The temporary repairs Maxim and I affected earlier have failed, and once again the connecting walkway is exposed to vacuum."

Zephyr looks down at her station, then back at Wil, and adjusts the main viewer. "Wil, look at the remnants of the anti-Peacekeeper fleet. They're breaking away from the carriers."

"Can't blame 'em. This looks like a lost cause."

There are only ten ships left, out of the nearly forty that had first rallied to attack the Peacekeepers. All of them seem to have sustained at least some damage. A few will likely be destined for the scrapyard, assuming they survive even that long. The three remaining Peace-keeper Carriers are still giving chase. Two of them are damaged, but not enough to give up their pursuit. The third, having taken a rear-guard position, is entirely untouched.

The *Ghost*, on the other hand, is not in great shape. One engine is completely gone. Apart from the sub-light drive functioning at only half power, there are also several breaches in the hull: some patched, some not.

"No," Zephyr says, pointing at the screen. "They're coming this way!" No sooner has she spoken than the ships in the display pass over and under the aft camera, and several loud clunks can be heard from the top and bottom of the ship. The whole ship shakes slightly; this is not the jarring impacts of weapons fire, but something else. "They're locking on to us with grapplers."

Wil looks at his console, and sees their speed increasing, climbing back up to full sub-light. He frowns.

"I can't believe it. They're towing us to Harrith Prime. What're they doing?"

Maxim looks at his tactical display. "Following. The third ship, the least damaged, is moving into the lead, and accelerating rapidly.

We're not in the clear yet. We're still at least a tock from Harrith Prime, and that ship will overtake us in half that time."

"We're being hailed," Zephyr announces.

"Please tell me it's not the Peacekeepers," Wil says, looking over at her. There's nothing to focus on, now that even the flight of the *Ghost* is out of his hands.

"It's a Harrith ship. It's Commander Shre' ta'n." Zephyr is smiling, probably just as glad as Wil is to know that the one friendly face they've encountered so far is still alive.

"On screen." A second later, through the static of the primary display, Wil sees the commander. She looks exactly like Wil feels. Her bridge is smoky and chaotic, and there's what looks like a med team tending to a fallen crew member in the background. "Commander Shre' ta'n,: he says. "It's good to see you with us still."

"You too, Captain Calder. Your ship is a testament to Ankarran shipbuilding and your expert piloting. The Peacekeepers are not giving up, I presume because you have the original source of that data packet on your ship?"

"That, and two eye-witness ex-Peacekeepers, who can testify to seeing documents relating to this whole thing. Do you have a plan? Is your government getting involved?" Wil leans forward in his chair. "We saw that there's a GNO reporter out here somewhere. She's seen the data, I assume?"

"The Harrith government is getting involved, yes. I've been informed that our diplomats on Tarsis are causing quite a stir at the GC assembly building. Also, I've been instructed to ensure the safe arrival of your ship on Harrith Prime." She stops, looking over her shoulder. The audio must be muted on her end, because she starts talking but Wil can't hear anything. She turns back to the screen. "The Peacekeepers seem intent on doing what they can to eliminate all evidence of this little dren-storm they've caused. To answer your question: yes, the GNO reporter is aboard one of the Quilant cruisers. We hope that her continued updates will force the Peacekeepers to withdraw."

Wil smiles. "Hope you're not holding your breath, ma'am."

The Commander seems confused. "Why would I do that?"

"Never mind, it's just an expression on my planet. So what's the plan? We're out of the fight—our weapons are all offline. Our main reactor is only operating at fifty percent. We're dead weight."

"Is your space frame intact enough for a short trip at FTL?" the Commander asks.

Wil looks over to Gabe, who nods. "Yes, Commander, the *Ghost* should survive a short trip at FTL."

She nods. "Then hold on to something."

The screen goes dark, and the ship lurches hard enough for the inertial compensators to flutter. Typically tied into the ship's systems and coordinated by the main computer, they haven't received the advanced warning they need to ramp up their efforts along with the ship's acceleration. Luckily for the crew of the *Ghost*, compensators work in fractions of fractions of ticks—and so, while unpleasant, the jump to FTL doesn't result in everyone on-board becoming salsa on the back wall of the bridge.

"Well, Xyrzix and Megan, I have to say that what started as a story of the GC and Peacekeepers stepping in to protect GC members from unaffiliated systems and rebels within those systems, has now turned into a story of corruption and greed among the upper ranks of the GC and Peacekeeper. Not only have we thoroughly reviewed the data packet released by Captain Wil Calder, but I've now heard— through the grapevine of this hodgepodge fleet—that aboard the *Ghost* are two ex-Peacekeeper officers who can testify to seeing several documents outlining this scheme to forcefully take over unaffiliated systems and join the GC under duress. Reports are that the original source of the incriminating recording is also located on board this ship."

Mon-El Furash pauses, to collect herself. "I'm still aboard the

Quilant cruiser that rescued the life pod I was in. The Quilant have formed a loose alliance with the Harrith Navy, the Zengar, and—surprisingly—the Harrith rebels who previously bombed two Quilant freighters. I'm told that high-level discussions among the ships' commanders have cleared up a lot of the misunderstandings between the two Harrith factions. I've also spoken to the Captain of this ship, and he informs me that the rest of this small fleet has agreed to protect the *Ghost*. Getting it to Harrith Prime, where presumably the ex-Peacekeepers from the *Ghost*—as well what we are presuming is the bot that originally recorded the secret conversation—can be debriefed and interviewed."

The newscaster stops and nods, as if listening to something, then continues. "Yes, at this time, at least out here, there's been no official word from the GC or this Peacekeeper taskforce. A Commander Janus, who's indicated he is in charge of the four new vessels that appeared, has only accepted one hail since his conversation with Captain Calder was re-broadcast."

Another pause, and then, "Yes, things are quieter right now. A few moments ago, the *Ghost*, likely in a last-ditch effort to buy itself time, launched a very powerful missile at the pursuing Peacekeeper ships, but rather than target one ship directly, they detonated the missile between two ships, doing what I'm told is only moderate damage to both. That said, however, the two damaged ships have slowed slightly, and the command ship has taken the lead in this chase. The allied fleet has disengaged from harassing the Peacekeepers, redirecting their efforts to surrounding the heavily damaged *Ghost*, which I for one am happy about. As always, I'll keep you posted as things develop here. This is Mon-El Furash with GNO, live from the developing situation on the frontier."

CHAPTER 16

HOME STRETCH

While it would have taken an hour or more to get to Harrith Prime at sub-light speed, it is only a twenty-centock trip at FTL. While this is underway, the entire crew, with nothing else to do, makes their way to the medbay to check on Bennie.

It is the first time since the battle started that Wil has been able to survey the damage to the *Ghost*. His spirits begin to fall the moment he leaves the bridge, which was a wreck but makes the rest of the ship look brand new. The main corridor connecting the forward section to the bulk of the ship is ravaged, a hastily-installed patch covering a meter-wide rip in the side. The faint wheeze of escaping oxygen can still be heard around the edges. Conduits and pipes are shredded— some patched and repaired, most not. The main crew space, lounge, and kitchenette, while intact, is a mess. A nearby section must have decompressed, because anything not bolted down has been blown around the space. The emergency bulkhead leading to the living quarters is closed, meaning that one or more of the crew berths has been exposed to space. Turning down the short corridor leading to the medbay, Wil sees more ruptured pipe and torn wiring.

The medbay, surprisingly, is in pretty good shape. The small space has only two beds, with the autodoc wedged between them.

Equipment overhead can seal off one or both beds into surgical suites, if necessary. Bennie is laying on one of the beds, the autodoc in standby mode beside him.

"He doesn't look too bad," Wil comments.

"Almost peaceful," Maxim says.

Zephyr checks the wall display set above the head of the bed, assessing Bennie's vitals. "Looks like he'll live. The autodoc set the broken bones and relieved the swelling in his brain. I guess that head wound was worse than I thought," she adds, almost a whisper. "Thank you, Maxim, for getting him down here."

Maxim looks from Bennie to Zephyr. "Of course. He's crew." He places his big hand on the small Brailack's leg.

Wil and Zephyr both nod. Wil walks around the bed and faces the two ex-Peacekeepers and the engineering bot. "Max is right: Bennie is, we all are, crew. Family. I haven't had that in a long time. I didn't leave my world and home system by choice. I was kidnapped and thrust into this life." At the questioning looks on the Palorians' faces and the head-tilt of the bot, he raises a hand, to hold off questions, "A story for another time, maybe. Suffice to say, in the last few cycles I've been dealing with homesickness, loneliness—and I'd guess some depression, as a result. But these last few weeks, I've felt more alive than ever. I didn't set out to have a crew this big. Max and Zephyr were supposed to be it—I had it all set out in my head. As they say, though, plans never survive first contact, and mine certainly didn't." He looks down at Bennie. "I've known Bennie longer than the rest of you. I'd never considered that he'd leave Fury, so he was never someone I considered asking to join me. Circumstances clearly had other plans.

"Whatever happens next, I want you three—and Bennie, when he wakes up—to know this. You're crew, you're family; the *Ghost* is and always will be your home." Wil looks at Maxim and Zephyr, now standing side-by-side holding hands, "You both know that I didn't want to get involved. I didn't know about any of this when I rescued you from the Partherians. But thank you for helping me see the right path and to do the right thing. Being out here on my own, doing some of the things I've had to do, seeing the things I've seen, I kinda lost track of that for a bit."

"Is this when we all hug?" Gabe asks.

Laughter breaks out from all three non-bot crew members, and they move to hug the tall robot.

From the speaker in the ceiling: "Attention crew, five minutes until arrival on Harrith Prime."

"Okay, team, show time. This isn't over yet. That Peacekeeper Carrier is most definitely behind us—possibly all three of them are. It's gonna be a fight. Gabe, I know there's not much you can do for our sub-light systems, but I have a feeling we'll be landing on the planet, so I'll need you in engineering, making sure our atmo-engines work."

"Captain, in case you have forgotten, the port engine pod is gone. And with it, the port repulsor lift. Atmospheric flight, let alone landing, will be tremendously difficult, if not impossible," Gabe warns.

"Shit, I forgot, actually. Well, it is what it is. I don't think we'll be safe until we're on the ground. That Peacekeeper Carrier on its own could likely destroy whatever space stations the Harrith have."

Zephyr turns. "Do you think Janus would go that far?"

"You know him better than I do, but yeah, I think he might." Wil sighs. "The cat is out of the bag, but if he can destroy the evidence and the witnesses, it all becomes circumstantial. The GC isn't going to explain this away easily, but they have the resources to make this all look like a gigantic hoax. We have to keep that from happening."

The drop from FTL to sub-light is rougher than normal, but considering that the *Ghost* is no longer operating under its own power, this is not surprising. The moment they return to normal space, Wil throws the throttle as far forward as it will go, knowing that only about fifty percent of his top speed is available. The ships that were towing the *Ghost* have detached and are now breaking off, circling back around toward the lone Peacekeeper Carrier that has dropped out of FTL directly behind them.

"Incoming message from Commander Shre' ta'n," Zephyr announces, putting the message through on the primary display.

"Commander," Wil greets her.

"Captain, you need to get to the main spaceport at the capitol. Harrith Space Control will be calling shortly. The rest of us will cover you. We hope that this Commander Janus will give up once you're clearly out of his grasp. The Quilant Cruiser with the GNO reporter will stay to the side, to capture as much of the proceedings as possible. Good luck." Without waiting for Wil to acknowledge, the screen goes blank, then returns to its default view of the planet below them.

"Incoming missiles," Maxim announces. "Fleet is maneuvering to intercept."

"Going evasive! Well as evasive as we can," Wil amends.

"Incoming hail from Harrith Space Control," Zephyr announces, then puts through the call on the primary display.

A young Harrith in a Harrith Navy uniform shows on screen. "*Ghost*, this is Harrith Space Control. We've cleared the airspace over and around Sha'Kri spaceport. Do you require any other assistance?"

"Hey there, Harrith Space Control, that's mighty nice of ya, and we appreciate it. We will most definitely need help. Our port engine pod is damaged. Well, okay, it's actually mostly gone. That leaves us one repulsor lift shy of what we need for atmospheric flight. Our atmo-engines are functional, but this ship isn't designed to fly on lift alone I'm afraid." Wil is fighting the controls and jerking the ship left and right as best he can, to avoid as much fire as possible. Thankfully, a Zengar frigate has taken up position above and behind the *Ghost*, using its shields to protect the smaller craft, mostly.

The young officer nods. "Acknowledged, *Ghost*. We'll dispatch a landing assist drone. It will meet you once you clear the outer atmosphere. Unfortunately, they're not designed for re-entry, so you'll have to get there on your own, but after that it'll link up with your ship's computer and attach itself to your port side."

The ship rattles, skimming the upper atmosphere. "Acknowledged and thanks!" Wil says, focusing on his controls. The primary display resumes the default view, a rapidly-growing planet directly ahead and below the ship.

"Okay, everyone, hang on to something! Gabe, we good on the atmos?"

Overhead the reply comes back, garbled and barely coherent: "Yes, Captain. The atmospheric engines are ready to go. I've also diverted all remaining shield power to the forward shields."

"Good call!" Wil has both hands on the flight controls. Maxim and Zephyr are hanging on to their stations tightly. On the primary display, the planet is becoming obscured by the superheated plasma forming along the deflector shields. The ship is rattling non-stop now, and shaking violently.

Behind the ship, the battle hasn't stopped raging. The Peace-keeper Carrier is plummeting toward the upper atmosphere, being harried at every turn by the few remaining ships capable of fighting, including the Quilant ship assigned to hold back to ensure a recording of the battle survives. A damaged Zengar frigate plows directly into the Carrier, exploding and causing explosions all along the side of the ship. The Peacekeeper craft is unloading every missile battery it has, swamping the shields and defensive capabilities of the defenders. A Quilant ship explodes right next to a Harrith rebel cruiser, which then also explodes.

"This is Mon-El Furash, with GNO, for what might be my last report!" The lights around the newscaster flicker, and smoke is visible everywhere. "The Quilant cruiser we were on originally was going to stay on the sidelines to ensure a record of this... incident... is captured, but the Peacekeeper Carrier has devastated the defenders to the point that this very cruiser is one of the few left to bravely defend the *Ghost*. As you can see, we've taken a lot of damage, and I've heard there are massive casualties across the ship. I'm told the few remaining vessels that helped the *Ghost* into FTL to make the trip to Harrith Prime have had their numbers cut in half already." She ducks off screen as sparks erupt nearby.

"I'm not sure if this vessel will survive this engagement, but as long as the truth is revealed, I've done my job! Back to you in the studio!"

ANY LANDING YOU CAN WALK
AWAY FROM

As the primary display clears, and the planet below comes into focus, Wil can see cities covering much of the terrain, with large green spaces and forests spanning the gaps—just kilometer after kilometer of green and growing things. Wil whistles appreciatively at the sight.

"Incoming contact," Maxim reports.

"The flight assist drone?" Wil has only ever seen a drone like this in use once. A freighter on its approach to a spaceport he happened to be docked at had experienced a blow-out in one of its repulsors—probably, based on the appearance of the freighter, from neglecting regular maintenance. The spaceport had scrambled a flight assist drone—two, actually, in case the first suffered damage.

Flight assist drones are little more than large repulsor systems with basic AI capabilities, which help get them close to the target and locked on. Once attached, the AI shuts down and shunts all control to the ship its assisting via a slave circuit. From that point forward, the drone is little more than a slightly ugly repulsor grav-locked onto the vessel. Once the ship is on the ground, the drone AI re-activates and takes control, flying back to its base of operations.

"Looks like it. I've never actually seen one, but yeah, that must be it," the big Palorian replies.

Wil glances over to Zephyr. "Hail it and guide it in. I'm a bit busy. If you need something, call out—otherwise, I'm going to do my best to keep us moving in a straight line."

The drone is moving fast toward the *Ghost* and only slows as the gap between them closes. By the time the *Ghost* screams past overhead, the drone is almost matching its velocity. Zephyr has opened a comm link to the pilot AI, and she is guiding it in, helping to identify hard points on the hull that the drone can attach itself to.

"Sending you a velocity adjustment!" she shouts.

"Acknowledged," Wil replies, making the changes needed. Seconds later, the sound of something large latching onto the ship reverberates throughout. Momentarily, the controls go sluggish, due to the substantial increase in weight and drag the drone has suddenly added. But within another second, the main control display shows a repulsor active where the port engine should be, completely slaved into the *Ghost*'s central control systems. "Okay, this is kinda cool!" Wil says, adjusting power between the two repulsors and the atmospheric engines.

Only minutes later, they're approaching the spaceport. Their target landing pad is right out front of the administration center. Several adjacent pads have been cleared. *Probably a good idea,* Wil thinks.

He's working the controls to slow the *Ghost* down, still about a kilometer from the spaceport, when Maxim shouts something that's lost in the sound of explosions and metal tearing. Four missiles, launched from the Peacekeeper Carrier at an angle impossible for the defenders to intercept, have taken a wide course through the atmosphere to eventually collide with the *Ghost* on its final approach. The flight assist drone is gone, Wil gathers, as is the starboard engine pod and its repulsor. The port atmospheric engine is also offline—he can't tell if it's there, or gone.

"Hang on!" he shouts, slamming the throttle for the atmo-engines to full power. A loud boom resonates through the ship, as the lone engine pushes the *Ghost* up to supersonic speed. Everyone is slammed back in their seats, as the *Ghost*—which had for one second been falling like a rock—is now falling more forward than downward, though technically it's still falling. "Brace!" Wil shouts, as the *Ghost* approaches the outer wall of the spaceport, barely clearing it. A loud scraping erupts from below; warnings go off everywhere, and the computer is saying something, but Wil can't hear over the noise of his ship screaming through the air.

Once past the outer wall, Wil cuts the power to the engines. The *Ghost*, still moving incredibly fast, drops to the ground below. The drop does little to slow the speed of the ship, which is now scraping and bouncing across the spaceport landing area, hitting random ships and bouncing like a pinball as it makes its way to the empty space that had been set aside for it. The entire bridge is dark now, the primary display first crackling with more static, then going dark, then finally—in a burst of hot metal and glass—shattering completely. The three crew members hold on for dear life, as their ship continues to bounce and slide across the landing area, leaving a tremendous gouge in its wake.

The *Ghost* finally comes to a slow wobbling halt, right in front of the main administration building. "At least we parked where they wanted us to," Wil says, then passes out.

Outside the ship, fire and rescue vessels are buzzing across the spaceport like angry insects, extinguishing fires all over the landing area, and the *Ghost* itself.

CHAPTER 17

AFTERMATH

Consciousness comes slowly: first, in fits and starts; then a moment that feels like wakening—then nothing. Then another fit of wakefulness, following by darkness again.

How long this continues is anyone's guess, at least from Wil's perspective, before the waking moments become more frequent and last longer. Voices drift in and out of his hearing—mostly sounds that aren't recognizable, but sometimes a voice that is. There's pain, too, so much pain, but there's no focus to it, like he remembers from broken bones, just an all-over, head-to-toe ache.

It starts as only a slightly less complete darkness. Then there's some haziness, before the haziness begins to take on shapes. At the same time the voices, both familiar and not, have returned. Gradually, the haze lessens.

"Uhhhhh..." Wil rasps out. "Did anyone... get the number of the dump truck... that sat on me?"

"What's a dump truck?" one of the familiar voices says. As the haze clears more, Wil can see there is a giant of a man next to his bed. *Maxim.*

"Oh... hey, Max." Wil's voice is a whisper, his throat is dry. "Water, anyone?"

He feels a straw touch his lips, and drinks down a small bit of water. His throat loosens; the dryness fades. He is slowly feeling more human—not that he recalls what that means, anymore. "Better."

Another familiar voice speaks: "Does this mean I can't have his quarters?" There's a shuffling, then a *thunk*, then the same voice, saying "Ouch!"

Wil grimaces. "He lived, huh?"

Bennie lets out a growl. "Nice to see you, too." He looks more or less intact, Wil can see now—the autodoc did a great job setting his broken bones, so instead of a cast on his arm and leg, he only has bandages.

Wil smiles, and blinks a few times; the haze retreats, the room coming back into focus. It's a hospital of some type. Zephyr and Maxim are there, Bennie too. But where's Gabe? There's also a nurse and a doctor—or at least, that's what Wil assumes they are—both Harrith.

"We're on Harrith Prime. We didn't die," Wil says. "At least, I hope we didn't die. Because if this is the afterlife, I want my money back."

"Do any of you know what he's talking about?" the doctor asks, looking around the room.

"We rarely do," Zephyr replies. "It's apparently a human thing?" She shrugs and reaches down to grasp Wil's forearm. "It's good to see you, Wil. We were worried there for a while. You were pretty beat up when they found us." She and Maxim both look fairly good, through a few scrapes and bruises are visible, almost healed, and Maxim has a bandage of some type on his arm and hand, mostly hidden by his shirt.

Wil looks around. "I don't remember anything after taking those missiles. What happened?"

The doctor, a tall Harrith woman, raises a hand to interrupt. "Captain Calder, I'm Doctor Shre' na'toth. You've been in a coma for five weeks. We honestly weren't sure you'd come out of it. We've never treated one of your kind before, and it seems neither has anyone in the sector." She consults the tablet she's holding, taps a few things. "As far as I can tell, you're fine now. We were able to repair the physical damage and hoped that the rest would work out. Not very scientific, but it was all we could do." She nods to Wil, as if pleased. "I'll come back later to check on you. I expect your crew has much to tell you." She turns to leave, the nurse following her.

Wil looks at Zephyr, trying to take it all in. "A coma? Five weeks?" She nods. "What happened? Where's Gabe?" He has a terrible thought. "Who's gonna pay for this?"

Zephyr pushes his leg aside and sits down on the bed. Maxim and Bennie drop into chairs they've pulled up beside the bed. "It's been an interesting few weeks, to say the least." She raises her hand to stop whatever Wil is about to say. "Gabe saved us. I can't say for certain who went down first, but what I know is that when Gabe forced his way onto the bridge, all three of us were unconscious. A large section of the ceiling had fallen on you, either before or after you passed out. He pulled all three of us out through the airlock, where the rescue crews were gathering, then went back in to get Bennie from the medbay. Don't worry—I can tell from the look on your face what you're thinking. Gabe is okay, he's with the ship overseeing the repairs. He stopped in to see you, then went to the spaceport. He hasn't left the ship since."

Wil smiles. "You coulda started with the whole 'Gabe is okay' thing."

Zephyr snorts. "I'm a warrior, not a storyteller. Shall I go on?" He nods. "Once we were on the ground and the rescue crews had us, Janus took his ship and fled. No one has seen him or his ship since— and they're looking, believe me. The Harrith have filed suit against the GC, as have the Zengar and the Quilant. The Peacekeepers have been recalled from most of their patrols and posts for review and overhaul. They're doing everything they can to save face. They've already publicly disavowed Janus and those identified in the data Gabe captured, or those I saw in the documents I stumbled on."

"But he hasn't surfaced? Aren't there, like, a few thousand people aboard a Peacekeeper Carrier? How could they all be on board with this plan?" Wil tries to sit up in bed.

"Peacekeepers are loyal," Maxim chimes in. "Sometimes to a fault. It's likely Janus and his conspirators have been planning this for a while, and that whole time he was shifting people around so that the most blindly loyal, and possibly corrupt, were aboard his ship. Those not loyal are likely floating in space somewhere."

Zephyr picks back up the story. "Commander Shre' ta'n and two other ships—one of them the Quilant vessel with the news woman on it—gave chase, but the Carrier jumped to FTL, and they lost it."

Bennie jumps up in his chair. "You forgot the part about the rebels!" Zephyr looks over at him and nods, and he grins, delighted with the chance to speak. "So, obviously, the rebels realized they were played, right? They joined in the fight after we transmitted our data—but that's not all! Once things got back here to Harrith Prime, the rebels rolled over completely. Apparently, whatever their goals, they weren't willing to put their people and system in more jeopardy. The rebel leaders on the moon hunted down every contact they had—contacts they now knew were Peacekeeper agents. Two days after we crashed here, a shuttle landed at the government compound with the rebel leaders and their prisoners. They turned themselves in, along with the Peacekeepers. The trial started last week!" The little hacker drops back in his seat, having made his contribution to the story.

Zephyr nods. "The GC and the Peacekeepers did their best not to let the trial proceed, but when two of their members—the Quilant and the Zengar—sent more ships to blockade the planet from Peacekeeper forces, the GC had no choice but to let the trial go forward. Of course, those agents have also been disavowed and left to their own defense." She shakes her head. "Deplorable, all of it."

NEW BEGINNINGS

For the next two weeks, Wil is confined to the hospital, where he is visited daily by his crew—apart from Gabe, who so far had only sent his well-wishes. Besides his team, his doctor has been his most constant visitor—mostly, he assumes, to learn as much as she can about humans. She's fond of poking him with things and measuring the response. He's thankful the poking hasn't been too invasive.

Mone-El Furash has also been to see him. Once with her camera-bot to record an official interview; the other times on her own, to collect background information. She had been a little banged up, too, and bore a few lingering bruises from her ordeal in space, but she seems to have taken the experience in her stride. Wil is hesitant to tell her too much about his world, especially with the GC and Peace-keepers in a state of turmoil. He doesn't want to risk anything happening to Earth because of all this.

On the day he's set to be released, he's visited by an elderly Harrith man in very nice clothes. The man closes the door behind himself before speaking.

"You're taller than I expected," he says by way of starting the conversation. Wil just stares blankly. "I'm Chancellor Tre'ta'nok. My people and I are in your debt, Captain Calder. I don't know if you grasp how close we were to giving in to the Peacekeepers and letting them take care of the rebellion. As I'm sure you know, that would have been the beginning of the end of Harrith autonomy. We avoided disaster, thanks to you." He bows, then walks over to the side of the bed, resting a hand on Wil's shoulder.

"I don't know how much your crew has told you, but I take our debt to you seriously. To start with, we have hired a small army of Ankarrans to come and repair your vessel. The Peacekeepers protested, a little, but it seemed the most logical place to start, and frankly from what I'm told was the only way to get your engineering bot to stop harassing the spaceport administrator." The old man smiles. "He can be quite a force, you know that?"

Wil smiles and nods. "I haven't known him that long, to be honest. But yeah, I am getting the sense that he's a force to be reckoned with."

"Agreeing to the repairs was, in fact, the only way he'd acquiesce to undergoing a forensic scan to validate the data packet you transmitted. Without him and your first officer, the case against the GC and Peacekeepers would be largely circumstantial. Of course, besides all that, we've covered the hospital bills for you and your crew, as well as room and board for them while they've waited for you to recover."

Wil nods. "Thank you. Thank you for taking care of them —of us."

"As I said, we owe you a debt, which in truth will never be repaid in full. It cannot be overstated how you secured the continued sovereignty of the Harrith people. That's not exactly a small thing," the old politician smiles. "At any rate, I know you are due to be released today, and I wanted to stop by and see you before the crowds get to you."

Wil makes a face, and the old man smiles.

"Oh, yes, did your crew not tell you? You're planetary heroes. There's been a crowd outside this hospital for weeks. Ever since it was leaked that this was the facility where the crew of the *Ghost* was being treated. I suspect your Brailack friend might have had something to do with that."

"A leak, huh?" Wil smiles. "I'm guessing this crowd has been helpful in stoking the anti-GC fires you've needed for the trials, here and on Tarsis?"

"Are all humans so insightful?"

"Something like that," Wil laughs.

"Well, young man, I will take my leave. I'm sure your crew is here to take you to the spaceport. The Ankarrans are quite fast at their work, I'm told." The old man turns and opens the door. Outside it Zephyr, Maxim, and Bennie are waiting, smiling.

Bennie rushes in. "Come on, let's go. Aren't you ready to leave yet?" He's pawing at Wil, tugging at him to get up.

Wil stands, with some difficulty, and grabs the duffel he has already packed. "I'm ready, I'm ready. Cut it out," he laughs, swatting away Bennies hands.

Chancellor Tre'ta'nok wasn't lying when he said there was a crowd outside the hospital. Easily a few thousand beings— mostly Harrith— are blocking the street, and several side streets in front of and near the hospital. Thankfully, Zephyr and Maxim have already mapped a way out of the hospital and into a ground car, which is parked a few blocks away.

The trip to the spaceport is thankfully quiet. No one sees them leave, so the crowd stay at the hospital, unaware. They have already called ahead, so the spaceport is ready when they arrive.

It hasn't occurred to Wil to ask, and no one has mentioned it, but now as the car enters the spaceport grounds, passing roadblocks and work crews, Wil sees for the first time how much damage has been done. Nearly a kilometer away, at the far end of the spaceport, a section of the main retaining wall is broken and crumbling, only recently covered in reinforcing mesh by work crews. The gouge that marks the path the *Ghost* had taken is still visible, but in most places now as just a section of fresh duracrete and paint.

As they come around a work truck of some type, Wil sees it. His breath catches in his throat, and he lets out a kind of sobbing, choking noise. Bennie looks at him with some worry. "Maybe he's not better?"

Wil smiles. "I'm fine, I'm fine. I just can't believe it. She's more beautiful than ever." Tears are freely flowing down his face.

They get out of the car together, and walk toward the *Ghost*.

She's no longer resting on her lower hull, but sitting on the deployed landing gear. The port engine pod is where it should be, attached to the ship. The various rents and gashes that Wil knows once existed are all gone. The forward section isn't crumpled and dented. The cargo ramp leads to an intact cargo hold.

Wil lets out a low whistle. The entire hull is unblemished—even dings and dents that existed before this whole adventure started are gone. It's like the Ankarrans built an entirely new ship, instead of repairing the one he had.

"Where are they?" he asks. "The Ankarrans?"

"They left two days ago," Maxim answers. "Not a very chatty bunch. We tried to get them to stay so you could thank them in person. They declined."

From the top of the cargo ramp comes a voice. "Hello, Captain. I hope you will forgive me for not coming to see you in the hospital more frequently. As an engineer, there was nothing for me to do there, and plenty for me to do here."

Gabe starts to walk down the cargo ramp. Wil walks up to meet him, and puts his hand on the big bot's shoulder. "I understand. Thank you for looking after her."

Gabe bows slightly. "Of course."

"Well, Megan and Xyrzix, things are certainly getting interesting. I'm still on Harrith Prime, for what some are calling the trial of the century. The accused Peacekeeper agents are taking the stand tomorrow, and it's anyone's guess what they'll say. They've been publicly disavowed by both the Peacekeepers and the GC, but have maintained their innocence, saying they were just following orders from their superiors." Mon-El Furash is standing outside a building amid a large crowd of protesters and reporters a like. "As this trial is hitting a critical phase, the hunt for the renegade Peacekeeper, Commander Janus, and his ship have so far turned up nothing. Some say that this is further Peacekeeper interference and that the ship has been located but the Peacekeepers just aren't telling anyone. Who can say, at this point, which is the more likely scenario?" She pauses, listening to something in her earpiece. "Yes, that's correct. The last member of the crew of the *Ghost*, its Captain Wil Calder, has been released from the hospital and is reportedly at the spaceport now. I say reportedly because, somehow, despite the sizable crowd around the hospital, Calder and his team have not been seen coming or going. I suspect they're trying their best to avoid the limelight right now."

NEW DAY, SAME PROBLEMS

Wil wakes up, thankfully in his own bed, in his quarters aboard the *Ghost*. It's been a week since his release from the hospital, and he's anxious to get on with his life. Despite the Ankarrans leaving, the *Ghost* wasn't exactly ready to fly. Gabe had a few more things to do that the Ankarrans deemed within his abilities to manage without them. Plus, there was the little issue of explaining the existence of the XPX-1900 missile still in the *Ghost's* magazine.

The crowd from the hospital hadn't taken long to relocate to the spaceport. Thankfully, the local police and armed forces are keeping a secure perimeter, since technically the port is closed while the repairs to its structure are being completed. Traffic is being diverted to two other spaceports nearby.

Wil walks into the main crew lounge to find all the others at the table, eating breakfast. Bennie looks up. "Morning, sleepy."

Wil grunts and makes his way to the coffee machine. Out of habit, he reaches out to hit it a few times, before remembering that Gabe has fixed it. It makes coffee now without abuse. He takes a sip from the steaming cup that is dispensed, then another and sits down next to Bennie. "Okay, now I can deal with you." Bennie makes a discourteous grunt.

Just then, the computer speaks up. "Captain, there's an incoming message for you, from a Mr. Xarrix."

"Well, shit," Wil sighs, looking up at the ceiling. "Take a message."

A moment later, the computer chirps, "He says you owe him, and you're not off the hook."

Wil looks around the table. "Guess we'd better get going, so."

"Wil Calder, you grolacking krebnack! You're dead, you hear me! That little stunt you pulled at Harrith Prime almost ruined me! The data I went to great lengths to steal is worthless now—my operations on Malkor are in shambles, and the consortium somehow has the idea that I'm behind the break-in at their secure storage station. Thankfully, I was able to deflect that last charge a little, by giving an anonymous tip about the real identity of the burglars. Good luck, you're going to need it!"

"Good morning, I'm Mon-El Furash, coming to you live from the Harrith Prime central courthouse. The 'Peacekeeper Eight', as they're being called, have been found guilty on all counts. The verdict was read moments ago and, as you can hear, the crowd outside the courthouse is elated. The convicted Peacekeeper agents will be sentenced later today, and it's assumed that they'll face the maximum punishment of life imprisonment at a labor camp, contributing to the overall good of Harrith Prime for the rest of their lives." She puts a hand to her ear, listening. "Yes, that's right, Megan. All eight were found guilty. No, the crew of the *Ghost* hasn't been seen since two of them testified a few days ago, but they are –" She pauses and looks skyward, where a roar can be heard. "Correction, they were, until just now, still here on Harrith Prime." Another pause to listen. "Yes,

I'm told the trials on Atrax Three brought by members of the GC are nearing their middle as well, with the defense set to begin its case any day now. Now that this trial has wrapped up, I'll be making my way to Tarsis to assist our team there in coverage. Back to you in the studio."

The *Ghost* is an ever-decreasing dot overhead, atmospheric engines roaring as it gains altitude.

The End.

THANK YOU

If you enjoyed Space Rogues, I'd love it if you left a review. Seriously, reviews are a big deal.
Reviews help readers find authors.

This is but the first adventure of the crew of the *Ghost*. I loved writing it and seeing these characters come alive on the page. There's so much more to come for Wil and the team, I can't wait to share with you!

Continue the adventure!
Get Space Rogues 2: Big Ship, Lots of Guns now!

Want to stay up to date on the happenings in the Galactic Commonwealth?

Sign up for my newsletter at
johnwilker.com/newsletter

Visit me online at
johnwilker.com
Facebook
Goodreads
Bookbub
Amazon

OTHER BOOKS BY JOHN WILKER

Space Rogues Universe (in story chronological order)

- Space Rogues 1: The Epic Adventures of Wil Calder, Space Smuggler (You're holding it)
- Merry Garthflak, Wil: A Space Rogues Short Story (buy it now)
- Space Rogues 2 (Buy it now)
- Space Rogues 3 (Buy it now)

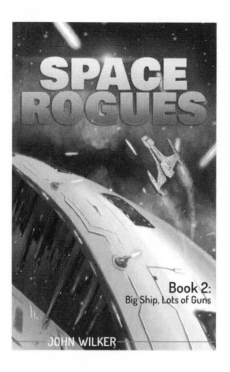

Please enjoy Chapter one of Space Rogues 2: Big Ship, Lots of Guns.

Or just get it now!

CHAPTER 1
SPACE ROGUES 2: BIG SHIP, LOTS OF GUNS

"Good morning from GNO stage fifty-nine on Artrax Three, I'm Mon-El Furash. The long-awaited closing arguments of the trial against the Galactic Commonwealth and the Peacekeepers has begun. It's been several months since this historic trial kicked off, following the incident at Harrith Prime that led to several member worlds of the Galactic Commonwealth filing a suit against the GC Governing Council as well as the top levels of Peacekeeper Command." The newscaster touches her large elephant-like ear, listening to someone. "That's correct, this trial has moved so slowly due to the sheer number of witnesses called and the time it has taken to assemble them—all while trying to ensure continuity of government here. It's been a long back and forth, and the outcome is still far from certain, but we'll all find out soon enough what the judges decide."

PRIVATEERING

"Okay, you know what, that was a lot of fun!" Bennie exclaims, a grin splitting his green face, entering the bridge of the *Ghost*. Behind him, Wil and Zephyr follow, both exhibiting a little bounce in their step. Zephyr is also smiling broadly.

Wil drops into his command chair in the center of the room, running a hand through his light brown hair. *Might be time for a haircut.* "No argument there. Those idiots got in way over their heads," he says, tapping a few commands into the control on the arm of his chair. "Between the reward and what we got from their hold," he looks down at the ship's account balance, "we should be able to pay off the bounty the Consortium put on our heads in no time."

Bennie cackles, and in a mocking voice says, "The Xenetan pirates are known throughout this sector, blah blah blah." He drops to the ground, kneeling, and cries out, "Don't hurt us! Please! Mercy!" Then he doubles over, laughing.

Zephyr takes her seat, bringing her own console to life. "I'll admit, getting a letter of Marque from the Harrith government has proven to be less of a terrible idea than I first assumed. There is something satisfying in kicking pirate ass, as Wil would say." She reaches up and releases her hair from the ponytail she prefers to use when in combat.

Wil beams. "So I was right? I'll take it." He leans back and puts his boots on the pilot station in front of him. "Bennie, what's up next?"

The small Brailack gets up from the floor and hurries to his console. He swipes the screen a few times. "We've got a few options. There's a mining colony that's been harassed by pirates a few times, so they're asking for help. There's an agricultural settlement that's offering a pretty credit for some livestock transfer. There's a freighter convoy looking for some protection out in the badlands, and a few other things on the network." A few more swipes. "The livestock job actually has the highest guaranteed pay-out."

The hatch to the bridge opens, and Maxim walks in. "I've secured the last of the crates we took on, what's next?"

Before Wil can answer, Zephyr does: "Livestock."

Without another word, Maxim turns and leaves the bridge.

"I know what he means," Zephyr says, looking from Bennie to Wil. "Livestock jobs suck."

Wil nods. "No argument here. Maybe that mining colony?"

Inclining her head, "Probably a good one. If it's pirates, we get to claim whatever is in their hold, plus fees." She smiles. "And their ship, those always fetch a good price."

Nodding, Wil says, "Yeah. Okay, Bennie, take the mining colony gig."

The Brailack nods. "Roger that." A few taps and then, "Okay, I'm sending the nav plot to your station. The colony is about three days from here, a small system called... well it doesn't appear to have a name, just a registration number. 'P3X-984', how poetic."

Wil nods. He flips a few switches and a low rumble begins to build from deep within the ship. Moments later, the *Ghost* is on its way. The station they have been docked at, in orbit over the outermost planet in the Harrith system, quickly recedes from view on the main screen. "We can go FTL in twenty minutes." He turns to

Bennie, "Why don't you go down and set the table? We'll get dinner going as soon as we hit FTL, and if I recall, it's your turn."

"It was my turn last night!" the small Brailack protests

"No, it wasn't. It was mine, and you know it," Zephyr says from her station, then sticks her tongue out at him, while pulling one eyelid down with her finger. The small alien mutters something under his breath as he leaves the bridge.

As the *Ghost* clears the station, and the gravity well of the planet it's orbiting, the large FTL nacelles at the end of its wings power up. At the rear of each a red glow begins to form, then with a flash the *Ghost* jumps to FTL. Wil and Zephyr have worked in companionable silence, getting the ship ready for their next mission and filing the appropriate paperwork to close out their most recent adventure in privateering. The letter of Marque might be lucrative, but the paperwork is monstrous. They stand to leave the bridge and join the others in the lounge. Before they reach the hatch, Zephyr turns to Wil.

"You know we can't keep this up forever. Right?"

Wil sighs. "I know, but that dickhead Xarrix burned us good. The Consortium still has its members and their bounty hunters out for our heads, and the only thing keeping them at bay, even a little, is the Harrith government and our arrangement with them. We leave this region of space, and it's a free for all. Believe me, as soon as we have enough to pay the bounty, we'll pay it."

He continues: "Stealing Gabe from the gangster storage facility was still the right thing to do."

Zephyr nods. This isn't the first time the two of them—she acting in her mostly-official role as first officer—have had this conversation. When they had agreed to raid a secret space station for Xarrix, they hadn't known that a Peacekeeper Engineering bot would be aboard. It turned out that GBE-102002—Gabe—was carrying important data, proving that the Peacekeepers were conspiring to create a war in order to force several non-member systems to join the Galactic Commonwealth. The *Ghost*'s decision to expose this plot had kicked off what GNO were now dubbing the "Harrith Incident," a shoot-out that had eventually involved several major systems, the Peacekeepers and the rebels and which was still having significant repercussions throughout the galaxy.

"I know it was the right thing, Wil," Zephyr says. "And the crew does too, but that doesn't mean they're not getting restless. The other day I caught Bennie hacking the voting system on Galatea—for the 'fun of it' he said, but I suspect he's been taking on side work."

"That little..." Wil starts then takes a deep breath. "Yeah, I can't blame him, I guess. Fucking Xarrix, it's not our fault whatever deal he had set up for Gabe and the data he contained fell apart."

"It sort of is," she smiles.

"Well, yeah, but it's not like we could have just walked away. I mean I wanted to and all..." he trails off, then resumes. "You and Max's reputations and lives were on the line. Not to mention everyone back there on Harrith." He shrugs. "I wonder what he even had planned—it's not like what Gabe had was all that lucrative. Outside of maybe the GC and Peacekeepers paying to keep a lid on it."

"Don't underestimate how much they would have paid to do just that." She sighs. "Well, just keep this in mind: something is going to have to change sooner rather than later if you want to keep this crew together." She turns and opens the hatch leading off the bridge.

DINNER, INTERRUPTED

In the crew lounge, the rest of the team is either lounging in one of the comfortable chairs in the center of the room or sitting to one side, at the small kitchen table set against the wall. Bennie is puttering around the kitchenette area, singing something that sounds to Wil oddly like "Manic Monday" by the Bangles.

Gabe is the only one standing, his yellow optical sensors spinning and focusing, his smaller fine manipulator arms are tucked up against his torso where Wil has noticed he keeps them to be out of the way. In his seat nearby, Maxim has a bottle of grum and is flipping through news feeds on the main room display.

"So, what's for dinner?" Wil asks, grabbing two more grum from the fridge. He hands one to Zephyr before she walks over and takes a seat next to Maxim, her free hand finding his.

Bennie turns around, holding a large pan with something sizzling in it in his hands. "Fried melba fish." His face scrunches up. "Wait, no that's not it—tahlo! Tahlo fish, that's it."

Zephyr, Wil, and Maxim exchange a look from across the room. Maxim asks, "What's a tahlo fish?"

"I picked some up on Harrith Prime when we were there last. The merchant said it was a delicacy. Something about the lake they live in, chemicals and such. Somewhere in the northern reaches," he shrugs. "After that, I kind of tuned him out until I paid." He raises a hand just as Wil opens his mouth. "But. I had him send me a recipe with my receipt."

This mollifies Wil. At least with a recipe, Bennie isn't winging it, which is usually when things go wrong in the kitchen—typically with fire involved. Followed by intestinal distress for one or more members of the crew.

Since the "Harrith Incident," as GNO has dubbed it, the crew have enjoyed a reasonably comfortable life as privateers for the government of Harrith. The battle had severely reduced the size and power of the Harrith fleet, and the Quilant and Zengar fleets had suffered similarly. As a result, piracy and general lawlessness became the order of the day in the Harrith system and its outlying territories, as well as several smaller systems nearby. Opportunists from all over the quadrant had started setting up shop: raiding small colonies, attacking shipping routes, and more.

That was when the governments of the major systems in the region began offering letters of Marque to any ship that could show sufficient firepower to act in that system's interests. The *Ghost* was more than suited for this type of work, and the work itself resonated with the crew. For the last seven standard months, the *Ghost* has been crisscrossing the sectors of space around the Harrith system: protecting trade convoys and ore shipments, and even occasionally running freight, when the load (and payout) is right.

All told, there are several hundred small- to mid-size ships roaming the area, acting for one government or another. While law and order are not fully restored, the last few months have seen a drastic decrease in overall crime in the area. According to the local news outlets, it'll be several cycles before any of the major powers get back to full military strength. Despite the losses, Harrith and its unaffiliated neighbors have flat-out refused the aid of the Galactic Commonwealth.

Luckily, all that balances out the other issue facing the crew.

After the "Harrith Incident" and their theft of Gabe from the secret space station, the Consortium that owned station had somehow been clued in as to why they had been robbed and who set the job up. Xarrix had one shot to escape the blame and quickly took it, burning Wil and the crew of the *Ghost* without a second thought. Bounty hunters from all over the quadrant were now looking for the *Ghost*, and while it was no secret where they were, the Harrith government and Navy had made it clear that the *Ghost* was still quite popular and would remain wholly protected while in service to the people of Harrith Prime.

Wil watches Gabe, who has moved to the kitchenette to talk to Bennie. The two-meter-high droid deploys his smaller arms and begins taking dishes and returning them to their storage cabinets. He finishes the task quickly, four arms helps. He has a wash cloth draped over his left primary arm.

Suddenly, Gabe pauses. "Captain, we're receiving a distress call. Wideband." Everyone else immediately stops what they're doing.

Wil gets up and heads for the bridge, Zephyr, and Maxim on his heels. As they go, Gabe offers, "I've instructed the ship to alter course." The hatch out of the common space closes.

Bennie looks up at his mechanical friend. "Guess we're clearing the table," he says.

Gabe picks up the tray with the fish on it. "It would appear so. Is tahlo fish good reheated?"

CRIME DOESN'T PAY

As Wil approaches the bridge, the hatch opens automatically. The main screen is already displaying a tactical plot showing the source of the distress call and the *Ghost's* relative position and speed. Taking his seat at the command/pilot station, he announces, "We're on course." Zephyr and Maxim quickly take their places.

Zephyr taps out a few commands and is murmuring into the mic at her station—likely talking to the source of the distress call, Wil assumes. She looks over at him and nods, and the overhead speaker comes to life. "Please repeat last," She says louder than before.

"*This is freighter* Sartomo. *We're under attack, there are three freighters in our convoy. We're under attack! Help us!*"

Wil tilts his head up slightly—a habit he's never been able to shake, despite it being completely unnecessary, as the computer will pick up his voice no matter what he does with his head. "This is Captain Wil Calder of the *Ghost*. We're on our way, but we're..." he looks over to Zephyr, who shows the count by flashing both hands four times—luckily, Palorians have five fingers, or more accurately, three fingers and two thumbs. "...forty centocks out. Can you hold them off?"

Static fills the speakers momentarily, "*I think so—all three of us have defenses, but we won't last forever. Please hurry!*"

"We're on our way. I promise. Just hang in there." There's a soft beep, indicating that the channel is closed. Wil taps on an icon set into the arm of his chair, and says quickly, "Gabe, are you in engineering? I need more speed. Ramp up the reactor to one-twenty."

"I am, Captain," the droid's voice informs him. "But the reactor and the engines will not be able to sustain that level of power for long."

"They only need to last less than forty centocks. Do it."

The ship shudders, and even with the inertia compensators everyone feels a slight lurch and pressure pushing them back against their seats. "Acknowledged," says Gabe's voice. There is another soft beep—the channel closing.

Zephyr looks up from her station. "New ETA, twenty-five centocks."

Wil nods. "Max, get ready. I'll drop us out of FTL as close to on top of them as I can. You'll have to lock on and open fire as fast as you can. Zee, did the Captain of the *Sartomo* say how many attackers there were?"

She nods. "Yes. Four."

Wil whistles. "Tough odds. For them." He grins at Maxim, who grins back.

The next twenty-odd minutes drag on, everyone waiting tensely in their seats. At fifteen minutes out, the long-range sensors are able to start telling them what's going on up ahead: two, not three, icons representing freighters are clustered together, with three red triangles orbiting them, occasionally swooping in close then back out again. *Looks like the situation has changed quite a bit,* Wil thinks. He assumes that one of the freighters is out of commission, either destroyed or at least disabled enough to not register on the long-range scopes.

From the overhead speakers, Gabe's voice comes again: "Captain, the heat shielding on the reactor is becoming unstable. We have, at most, five more centocks before I have to bring the reactor back down below one hundred percent. Ideally closer to eighty percent. Beyond that, the reactor will scram, and we will be on emergency power." The level of detail is, as usual, perfect—Gabe takes his role as ship's engineer seriously, and Wil appreciates it.

"Acknowledged. Push it as far as you can, as long as you can, then dial it back. Just remember, we're going into combat, so we're going to need more, not less, power."

There is what sounds like a sigh. "Very well." A soft beep as the connection is closed.

Bennie, who had joined them on the bridge mid-way during the flight towards the battle, finally chimes in. "I'm picking up narrow-band comms, likely the pirates talking to each other. They're encrypted, of course."

Wil turns to the station Bennie has called home for almost a year. "Can you crack them?"

"Of course I can, but do we care what they're saying? It'll be easier to just jam their comms." He rubs his small hands together.

"Fine, do that, I really don't care as long as they're off balance." Wil taps a few controls and the display switches to the view directly ahead of the ship: currently the stretched-out stars of FTL travel.

"Two minutes. Zee, hail the *Sartomo*."

She nods and taps a few things on her console, then nods again. Wil speaks loudly towards the ceiling, "Hang in there, we're here." He motions to her with a slashing gesture of his hand, and hears the soft beep of a closed comms channel.

A slight lurch forward tells them that Gabe has reduced the power output of the main reactor significantly. A minute later, Wil slides the FTL control back to "sub-light," and the *Ghost* is immediately in the middle of the fray. Directly ahead and to port are the two remaining freighters, one venting drive plasma from a wound near its main engines. Slightly further ahead and to starboard are two of the three attackers. They're small combat craft, about half as big as the *Ghost*, but well armed—cutter class at best, Wil decides. Likely a crew of two or three, the rest of the ship probably just cargo hold and engines.

Maxim unleashes the forward weapons on the two craft. The turrets below and beside the bridge roar to life.

Wil nods to Zephyr. "Hail them."

On the screen in front of them, the plasma cannons mounted on the main engine pods stream lethal bolts of energy at the furthest pirate, while the forward weapons, mounted under the forward section of the ship, spit almost equally deadly fire at the nearer pirate.

Zephyr nods back. "Attacking craft," she says, her voice all business, despite the battle raging outside, "this is your only warning. Power down your engines and weapons, or be destroyed." Then there is the familiar soft beep, telling Wil the channel has been closed. "Bennie?" Zephyr asks.

"Their comms are jammed. If they want to talk to each other, they'll have to do it in the open, until they settle on a new frequency... that we'd hear them agree to and I could jam again." He grins.

A pair of missiles streaks out from the launchers on the *Ghost's* underside. They fly from the bottom of the view screen, splitting up and heading towards two of the pirates. The two attackers directly ahead explode. Maxim is grinning from ear to ear.

"Well done, Max!" Wil shouts.

THE PAST

"Well as jobs go, this one sucked," Wil says plopping down into the command chair on the bridge. From the hold comes a screeching moo-type sound, and Wil winces. "Computer, is there a way to dampen the sound from the cargo hold?"

"*Negative.*" The infuriatingly calm male voice replies.

"Shit." He pulls up the pre-flight checklist and starts getting ready to leave whatever this planet is called. "Computer, open a channel to Xarrix."

A soft beep announces the channel is open. A few seconds later comes a familiar raspy voice. "You have them?"

"Yeah, I got 'em. Whatever the hell 'they' are."

"They're expensive, that's what they are. You don't need to know more. How soon can you be here?"

Wil looks at his console. "Eight hours—er, uh, long ticks? No. Eight tocks. Yeah, tocks."

There's a loud, hissing sigh. "Fine."

The soft beep announces the connection has closed.

"Asshole," Wil says.

The *Ghost* lifts off the planet and accelerates out of the

atmosphere. It's powerful atmospheric engines roar, pushing it away from the planet. The smuggler that met Wil with the creatures covers his face and swears.

Once the ship's course is underway, Wil heads back to the hold. As soon as the personnel hatch opens, he's assaulted by a smell so bad he makes a gagging sound and almost pukes. The creatures below look up and let out a screeching *moo* sound. He shudders and walks down to the hold. Whatever these things are called, they're ugly: six stubby legs sprouting from a tubby tube-shaped body, covered in slightly sticky leathery skin. Three tails swish back and forth lazily. To Wil, the worst thing about them is their faces—four beady eyes set wide apart on a big, flat skull, above a completely toothless mouth.

Wil pushes through the shuffling animals to the port side of the hold, where he grabs some of the feed Xarrix's henchman gave him. He scoops it up and tosses it to the floor. The salamander-cows, as Wil has decided to call them, shuffle around. Long, prehensile tongues loll out and writhe on the floor looking for the pellets.

"That's disgusting!" Wil shouts, edging back to the hatch while trying to avoid salamander-cow saliva. He shuts the hatch and heads back to the lounge with a shudder.

Wil drops into one of the large chairs in the crew lounge, a grum in one hand, something like beef jerky in the other. "Computer, update on search routine, 'find Wil friends'?" He looks at the ceiling, waiting.

"*No results.*"

"Really?"

"*No humans have been reported within the sphere of the Galactic Commonwealth.*"

"Man! Why hasn't someone kidnapped anyone else from Earth? How can I be the only one?"

"*Unable to answer.*" Wil imagines a smug, beach tanned face smirking.

"Shut up!"

With six hours to go, he looks around the lounge. "Mr. Sulu, are we still on course?" He nods slowly a few times. "Good, good." He looks over to the couch-thing, also empty. "Commander Worf, weapons status?" More nodding, then Wil sighs, and says, "Good. Hope we won't need weapons to transport salamander-cows."

Made in the USA
Middletown, DE
04 April 2019